Sure, I was snooping where I had no business to, but their reaction seemed a bit over the top…

I scanned around the room and found stacks and reams of paper, cans of ink in various colors, and several hand-operated printing presses, large and tabletop models. In a wastebasket were wrinkled-up copies of the flyer that reprinted the disarmament story from the *LA Times*. I heard the creaking sound again, beyond another door to my left. Slowly, I tried the door and found it unlocked. I pressed my luck and crossed the threshold.

It was an industrial storeroom, filled with rows and shelves of chemical supplies and stacks of rubber tubing and plastic hoses. There was a battered, wooden office desk pushed up against a wall. The wall contained a Ridged Tool calendar and a couple of *Playboy* pinups; Miss July and Miss August of last year. The desk contained a locked drawer, which I unlocked with a conveniently located claw hammer. Inside the drawer, I found a pile of wallets and key chains. One of the wallets held a 1956 California driver's license issued to Johnny Sunset.

I thought I heard a car pull up in the parking lot out front, which is what distracted me from the creaking noise behind me. I felt a jarring thump in the back of my skull, as I vowed never to be excited by nothing again. I half turned, but got another, harder hit on the head for my effort. Fireworks went off behind my eyes and slowly faded, falling away into blackness.

After rescuing Annette Funicello's stand-in from the amorous clutches of Guy Williams in March 1959, Stan Wade, young, LA-based PI, gets a new, but secret assignment from his number-one client, Walt Disney. The elder cartoonist and filmmaker wants Stan to investigate a death at Edwards Air Force Base. The victim, who drowned while testing an outer-space uniform, was the eighth astronaut candidate for America's new space agency, NASA. Working out of his cramped office in the back of the Brown Derby restaurant where he's employed as a part-time "bouncer," Stan uncovers much more than a suspicious death…putting his own life—and the lives of those closest to him—in danger.

than he expected, and he barely escapes with his life. *Starfall* is filled with endearing characters, a solid well-thought-out plot, and plenty of edge-of-your-seat tension, along with touches of humor that make this a worthy addition to the series and a great read. ~ *Regan Murphy, Reviewer*

STARFALL

A Stan Wade LA PI Novel

John Hegenberger

A Black Opal Books Publication

GENRE: HISTORICAL SPY THRILLER/MYSTERY-DETECTIVE

This is a work of fiction. Names, places, characters and incidents are either the product of the author's imagination or are used fictitiously, and any resemblance to any actual persons, living or dead, businesses, organizations, events or locales is entirely coincidental. All trademarks, service marks, registered trademarks, and registered service marks are the property of their respective owners and are used herein for identification purposes only. The publisher does not have any control over or assume any responsibility for author or third-party websites or their contents.

STARFALL
Copyright © 2016 by John Hegenberger ~ A Stan Wade LA PI Novel
Cover Design by John Hegenberger
All cover art copyright © 2016
All Rights Reserved
Print ISBN: 978-1-626944-19-0

First Publication: FEBRUARY 2016

All rights reserved under the International and Pan-American Copyright Conventions. No part of this book may be reproduced or transmitted in any form or by any means, electronic or mechanical, including photocopying, recording, or by any information storage and retrieval system, without permission in writing from the publisher.

WARNING: The unauthorized reproduction or distribution of this copyrighted work is illegal. Criminal copyright infringement, including infringement without monetary gain, is investigated by the FBI and is punishable by up to 5 years in federal prison and a fine of $250,000. Anyone pirating our ebooks will be prosecuted to the fullest extent of the law and may be liable for each individual download resulting therefrom.

ABOUT THE PRINT VERSION: If you purchased a print version of this book without a cover, you should be aware that the book is stolen property. It was reported as "unsold and destroyed" to the publisher, and neither the author nor the publisher has received any payment for this "stripped book."

IF YOU FIND AN EBOOK OR PRINT VERSION OF THIS BOOK BEING SOLD OR SHARED ILLEGALLY, PLEASE REPORT IT TO: lpn@blackopalbooks.com

Published by Black Opal Books **http://www.blackopalbooks.com**

DEDICATION

To Daniel Stumpf, the landbound and first reader

"I go into all these problems only to point out that our later successes were due, in great part, to the fact that we spotted the glitches and other difficulties when we did and ironed them out." ~ John Glenn, *We Seven*, 1962

Let's all remember that what follows is a work of "faction" based entirely on the author's dreams, recollections, and speculations. None of the names have been changed to protect anyone. All of the events *almost* occurred exactly as reported.

PROLOGUE

March 1959:

I loved my job. I got threatened and shot at by the most interesting people. Today it would be another Hollywood star. Tomorrow? Maybe a mobster. Maybe a commie. Maybe even an astronaut. But today's assignment was to go and bring back a wayward starlet. Or so I'd assumed.

So I grabbed an early lunch and pointed my battered '53 Kaiser Manhattan toward Palm Springs, cruising east on highway 111, past Cathedral City and Palm Desert. Eventually, the road snaked up a hill of boulders and rattlers to a swell hideaway spot. The low ranch-style house was a combination of Spanish and modern. I parked next to a chartreuse Caddy and checked the license plates. A hot, dry wind blew off the mountains and lightly ruffled my hair. I hung my sunglasses on the rearview mirror and got out to approach the front entrance, listening to my footsteps crunch gravel.

I knocked, listened, and tried the door. It was part wood and part glass and all locked. I took off my jacket, held it to the glass, and struck it smartly with my right elbow. I reached in through the hole in the glass and opened the door. Now I could hear pulsating music coming from a room in the back of the house. I walked toward it.

She was dancing, arms and legs spread wide. A leopard-skin one-piece bathing suit. The pool on the terrace behind her moving body shimmered in the afternoon sun.

I lifted the needle from the LP on the stereo, and she staggered when the sound stopped, turning to raise a fit.

"All right, Annette." I sighed, jabbing a thumb over my left shoulder. "Party's over. Let's go."

She screeched and let fly with a heavy cut-glass tumbler that bounced off the wall behind me. I smelled expensive whiskey.

She charged forward with raised claws, so I lifted the record from the stereo and skimmed it at her, like one of those new Frisbees. It bounced off her shoulder, causing her to stop and stare at me in shock. I gently took hold of her right wrist, spun her around, and enfolded her tight until she stopped twisting and stomping. I nudged the phone receiver off the hook with my right knee and dialed "0" with my left forefinger.

From the corner of my eye, I saw Guy Williams come into the room, tightening an electric-blue bathrobe. I raised the phone receiver to his handsome face. He stepped back, smiled, and bowed graciously.

This tough-guy persona was working fine for me and I figured this was going to be one of my better assignments. "Hello, operator? Get me Disney Studios. Hollywood. Stan Wade calling."

CHAPTER 1

And now, all I wanted to do was collect my fee. Tuesday, March 24, 1959, I breezed through the gates of one of the biggest little movie and television production companies in town and parked in a visitor slot next to the four-story factory, complete with its own water tower. *They'll put ears on that thing one of these days.*

Here, across sun-washed Burbank acres, pirates and frontiersmen, cartoonists and cameramen, accountants and actors toiled daily under the benevolent guidance of "Uncle Walt."

I'd worked a couple of jobs in the past for him and was here to see again today about money. Inside the fun factory, I slurped cool water from a stainless-steel drinking fountain and pressed the elevator's "Up" button to ride to Disney's office. As the mirrored interior doors slid shut, my reflection nodded at me and almost cracked a smile. Brown eyes with an arching eyebrow, dark hair with a streak of white, average build with the average face of an average office worker. Only this average guy hated office work, preferring to be out in the field, or on the street, or just about anywhere, except in heavy LA traffic.

Walt, on the other hand, was a man of sixty, possibly a little more, and had a lot of powdery gray hair, a thin moustache, and a handsome dissipated face that was beginning to go pouchy. His suit was tan and his tie was brown. The exact opposite of mine. A white handkerchief peeped out of his breast pocket and the fingers of his right hand drummed the change in his pants pocket.

I jerked a pack of Luckies toward him so a couple cigarettes extended in his direction. "Worried about me?" He was a chain smoker and this was his brand. "By the way, isn't Annette still under age?"

He accepted a smoke and lit up from a desk lighter shaped like the Nautilus submarine—the one from his movie, not the one that went under the North Pole last year. "She's twenty-one." He exhaled. "And some security analyst you are. Didn't you figure out during the long drive back that the girl I sent you after is really just her stand in?"

I wasn't sure I believed him. He'd kidded me before,

so I gave him my poker face. "Professional investigator, if you don't mind."

He took a deep drag, saying, "That still means you're only a PI. Hell, Stan, you need to think bigger. Quicker, too."

"Walt, she sat in the back seat the whole time and wouldn't talk. I dropped her off at the front gate and she stomped in without a word. Besides, you should know by now that I always get results when you hire me."

He stared for a moment at a framed photo on the wall beside a potted ficus. It was an old tintype of a steam engine crossing a high wooden trestle. "Maybe," he allowed.

"Look, you sent me out there and I brought her back alive and kicking. Scratching, too."

He let that go and rested a hip on the side of his desk. "She does Christmas parades and other events for us, where the public can't get close enough to tell the difference. Still, we can't have her running loose, like that. Bad for the company's overall image. Thanks for bringing her back, Stan. And thanks, too, for helping Fess with that blackmail thing last month."

I shrugged. "Always a pleasure. Just pay my bill and I'll be glad to keep watch over any of your cowboy heroes, anytime you ask."

"Humph. I've got another kind of hero that I want you to work on." My number one client went back around behind his desk and settled easily into a high-backed chair. "I have a featurette in development about weather satellites and another one about Project Mercury."

"Okaaaay." I'd read a little in the *LA Times* about the orbiting satellites which could track and maybe someday influence the weather. Sounded pretty far out there, literally. I'd also read about the test pilots that our country was assembling for the august challenge called Project Mercury.

Every branch of the military was being evaluated as part of America's program to launch a man high into the upper atmosphere, where he'd circle—scratch that—orbit the earth. If he was lucky, like that Russian had been, he'd come down in one working piece. I had to admit, it was a hell of an idea. The slide-rule boys insisted that we needed to do it or the Soviets would take over the world from on high and maybe even stake claim to the moon. Yep, pretty far out.

Walt got back up and straightened a picture on the wall that, as far as I could see, didn't need straightening. He mashed out his cigarette in an owl-shaped ashtray on his desk.

"You're still worried," I said, waiting him out. "What's all this space stuff got to do with you, anyhow?"

From a desk drawer, he pulled out his own pack of Luckies and lit up again. "I'm not going to get into that right now, Stan. Suffice it to say that I've got a heavy investment in it. I need you to go up to Edwards Air Force

Base to meet with Colonel Fielding Scott." He nudged a sheet of paper toward me across the polished surface of his desk. "He'll be expecting you. This will get you access to the base."

I scanned the paper. There was no indication that it came from Walt. It began and ended with a string of numbers like a coded telegram or a Christmas club account at the savings and loan.

"I still don't get it," I said. "All this for a space movie? Why am I meeting this guy?"

"In the past, when I've hired you, you've been discreet. I value the fact that you didn't ask me dumb questions."

"For a hundred dollars a day, plus expenses, right?" I wondered if he noticed that I'd just asked a question.

"Yes, well, we'll talk about those expense reports later." He gave me a lean grin, and I wished that it had been broader. "What I need now is an objective and confidential investigation into the death of a Mercury Project test pilot. You'll act under my direction and report back the details, plus whatever insight your investigation generates."

"Wait, now. Slow down." I held up my right hand—the one I used to scratch my head when I was confused. "Is this for real or are we talking about one of your movies? Who's dead and how?"

"I'm not the one you should be questioning," he said. "But the pilot's name is, or was, Albert Taffe. He was an air force captain stationed at Edwards, where he drowned."

"Drowned? Edwards is on the edge of the Mojave Desert."

Walt stared at me like he needed an antacid.

"Oh," I said quickly, "that's *why* you want me to investiga—"

An angry *buzz* sounded from an intercom box on his desk and a sweet Southern drawl said, "The people from ABC have arrived for your meeting."

Walt pushed a button on the box. "Put them in conference room B, Tommie. And let them know that I'll be right there." He snuffed out his smoke in the owl as I hesitantly got up to leave. "You have my private phone number, Stan. See Tommie for your check. You'll get the rest of details from Colonel Scott. Bring them back to me, along with your insights."

At the moment, my insights needed a telescope.

CHAPTER 2

On the drive back from the Magic Kingdom, I stopped at a local bank and cashed Walt's check. Back in the car, Alvin and the Chipmunks were warbling a silly tune on the radio. I was so busy thinking about my client's weird tale that I almost didn't notice the "D" missing from the end of the Hollywood sign up on Mount Lee. Some trained observer, I was.

I drove south and west along the surface streets and finally parked my Kaiser next to the trashcans in the lot behind the Brown Derby at Wilshire and Alexandria. Like Grauman's Chinese theater and the arch entrance to Paramount Studios, the big hat of the Derby restaurant was a local landmark. We're big on landmarks here in Hollywoo.

I walked past the smell of rotting lettuce and through the employee's entrance into a kitchen bustling with lunch chaos. As I reached the door to my cubbyhole office, situated between the wall of time cards and the washroom, I glanced into the main office and saw Cynthia's blonde hair covering half of her face. She was concentrating on a long adding machine tape and cradling the phone receiver between her left shoulder and her cute chin. I gave a quiet whistle and she looked up, almost losing the phone, then smiling and waving a pencil back at me. I smiled, too, and hummed a nonsense tune to myself while unlocking my cubbyhole.

The floor was littered with letters that had been shoved under the door. I scooped them up and eased around the side of my desk. I lit a cigarette and started opening the mail. Someone wanted me to subscribe to a magazine. Someone else wanted me to contribute to a charity fund. It was nice to be wanted, but I was tied up on a case now and didn't have the time. I wadded the junk mail into a ball and realized another thing I still didn't have: a wastebasket. I dropped the wad into a bottom desk drawer and pushed it shut with my foot, just as Cynthia popped her head in to the office to remind me that Carlo wanted the rent.

I'd been working out of the back of the Derby for the last couple of months, ever since a fire burned down my old office and most of the Farraday Building on Hoover near Ninth, about ten blocks away. Carlos Navarro—no relation to the actor—assistant manager of the BD had hired me at the end of last year to help deal with a union dispute that threatened to close the place down. The employees loved working where the sign said you could "Eat in the Hat," because they got great medical benefits. Also, they got great tips from the celebs who were regular patrons. But the union had a beef about the low hourly wages and planned to have the place picketed, until I stepped in and helped negotiations. We eventually worked out a deal where the union leaders could eat, but not drink, for free at any of the Derbies—there were three in town—so everybody wound up happy, for now. Then, when the fire barbequed my old office, Carlos had taken me on retainer here to collect unpaid restaurant receipts from a few deadbeat "stars" and I'd changed my mailing address to a cramped, windowless room at 3377 Wilshire Boulevard. I wasn't exactly a bouncer—more of an enforcer.

I told Cynthia that I'd just gotten paid and would be right over to her with the cash. "How about you and Jimmy joining me at a Dodgers game tonight?"

"Oh, I'd love to, Stan." Her blue eyes almost knocked me over. "But tonight is a school night and Jimmy can't afford to miss any more time, unless it's for a good reason."

I crushed out my smoke and waved the air. "How's he doing with his asthma?"

She brightened her smile. "Okay, now that he's stated taking the shots. He lost a lot of school time, Stan. You understand."

"Sure." I smiled back. I, too, suffered from a mild condition due to the city's abundant air pollution, but I didn't want to tell her about it.

She started to leave and then I saw her remember something. "Oh, Lex called and said she was going to start working on the engine and you're to bring supper."

"Okay. Thanks."

"And your friend from the TV repair shop is here, if you want to see him."

I knew who she meant, but said "You mean Weirick?" in order to keep her with me a minute longer.

"Uh-huh. He's having vichyssoise in the coffee shop. He's a weirdo."

"Thanks, Cindy." I needed to talk with Norman. "And don't let him hear you call him that."

"What? Weirdo? Oh my god, is that his real name?"

I eased past, giving her shoulder a pat and handing her four twenties. "This should cover what I owe Carlos. Maybe we can catch a ballgame this weekend."

"Sounds charming." She dazzled me again with her smile. "I'll get back to you."

As I walked through the main dining area, I realized that her answer didn't necessarily mean "Yes."

The Derby was crowded with noontime patrons. Every plush, shoulder-high booth was filled with people trying to see and be seen by other people. I spotted Gisele

MacKenzie with Art Carney. Yakima Canutt with Bob Steele. Rock Hudson with some handsome guy I didn't know. Lee J. Cobb was eating a salad that wasn't named after him, while above them all, on the "Wall of Fame," were framed caricature sketches of Hollywood royalty. Garbo, Gable, Gerson, and Groucho. The sketch of Durante and his nose took up two frames.

As I entered the coffee shop, I saw Norman seated at the lunch counter, reading a paperback book and finishing his soup. What I knew about outer space and the Mercury Project, you could stick in your hat, but I was confident that Norman could fill me in.

He was the smartest guy I know. Only trouble was that his smarts ran to electronic equipment and photography. He was a technical kind of guy of about nineteen—five foot four with sandy hair, poor complexion, and clamshell glasses. Most people who knew him said he'd rather spend time inside the solid-state chasse of a thirty-four-inch-wide Philco television than the solid chasse of a thirty-four-inch-wide girl named Phyllis. Personally, I thought they were being too hard on the guy, because Norman was an excellent employee who worked for the tightwad that owned the A-1 Electronics store on Melrose. I happened to know that he loved his job there, servicing and selling TVs, ham radios, and Japanese cameras. I also knew that he loved science fiction. He was a tad overweight and certainly over-informed when it came to scientific stuff. I liked the guy, even if he was a bit of a conspiracy nut, especially when it came to communists. We'd first met back in 1955 when I was working on a case for Roger Corman and Norm had been helping with the special effects on *It Conquered the World.*

I dropped onto the counter stool next to him. "Howdy, Norman."

He looked up from the book he was reading. *Eye in the Sky.* "Oh, hello, Mr. Wade. Guess what?"

"Coke and a cheese Danish," I told the brunette waitress behind the counter and then turned back to Norman. "What?"

"PKD is in town. Wanna meet him?"

It must have shown on my face that I had no idea who PKD was. Maybe he wanted it that way.

He leaned toward me. "You know? The guy I told you about who wrote *The Man who Japed.*" He waved the paperback at me and I got it.

"Phil K. Dick," I read off the cover. The name sounded faintly dirty, which surprised me about Norman.

"Right. Wanna meet him?"

"Maybe later, Norm. Right now I need some information."

He looked disappointed.

I went on. "I've got a new case involving astronauts and Project Mercury."

That perked his interest. "You mean NASA?"

I blinked at him. "No, Norm. Nassau is in the Bahamas, I think."

"No, no, Mr. Wade. NASA is the abbreviation of the National Aeronautics and Space Administration—the new civilian agency in charge of developing America's space program to put a man in orbit around the Earth."

"Sounds right—" The waitress came back with my Danish and a glass of Coke. I took a swig and almost choked on a tiny ice cube. She gave me a sympathetic smile and I gave her a buck for her trouble.

Norman watched her rear as it moved away farther down the counter. I didn't blame him. He turned back to me with, "Don't you read the papers?"

"I read Dick Tracy and Flash Gordon, but they have nothing to do with the real world."

"Wanna bet? Did you know that Edwards is home to the US Air Force Flight Test Center on Rogers Dry Lake, the largest natural aircraft landing field in the world? That's where they tested the XS-1 and now the X-15 in controlled hypersonic flight of more than five times the speed of sound."

I nibbled on my Danish while he filled me in with a few more facts. Finally, I asked, "How do you know all this, Norman?"

"Mostly from Willy Ley's column in *Galaxy* magazine."

Another faintly dirty name. "Who's Willy Ley?"

"You know? The guy who worked on the script for *Conquest of Space* and some of Disney's *Man in Space* TV shows."

"Oh, yeah. Him."

"Hey, Mr. Wade, speaking of writing. Do you wanna read the latest chapters of my Ninja Nazi Zombies novel?"

I'd fallen for that one before and knew better than to accept. "Like I said, Norm, I'm working a new assignment right now." I smiled. "Sounds charming, but I'll get back to you." If Cindy could say it, so could I.

❧❧❧

I hurried back through the main dining room, got my hat, locked up my cubbyhole, and drove my Manhattan west toward fresher air.

I pulled into the slot next to the pier where the cabin cruiser was docked on del Rey Lagoon, and gathered together the soggy bag of burgers and chicken-in-the-basket that I'd bought from a roller-skating carhop at the Galaxy Drive-in.

The Pacific Ocean looked flat as hammered metal and the setting sun had turned it a beautiful shade of burnt orange. I could smell the tang of seaweed and machine oil, and knew I was home.

They were dredging the lagoon to build the new marina, but it would be months, if not years, before the first yacht or schooner cruised in and laid anchor. At the edge of the seawall, I paused and listened to the wet gurgle of the tide, the insistent chang-chang of a halyard slapping against an aluminum mast, and the melancholy squawk of a seabird.

I crossed the gangplank, coming aboard the thirty-six-foot Taylorcraft cabin cruiser, past the wicker chairs and teak foredeck to the main hatch. From the below deck of the *Cervantes II*, I could hear a repeated thumping sound. I went down the ladder to be greeted with a warm, grinding growl from Lex Iglesia. "Hiya, squirrel. Gladda see ya."

Lex could have been called the more regal Alexis, or the more friendly Lexy, but she preferred the more mysterious and badass Lex. She was shorter and wider than I was with brown hair going to gray, red face and hands from the sun, and uninhibited opinions from practically everywhere else.

"When you gonna knock off this PI business and get a real job, like mine?" she asked in a voice like a cement mixer clearing its throat.

Not this again. I sighed and pushed a huge wrench aside to sit down on a worn wooden bench.

Lex had grown up in the '40s, not as a riveter, but as pipefitter's assistant from Kansas City, Kansas. She made sure that you knew it was not Kansas City, Missouri, because "that town was an eye-sore on God's good ass." She was built like a brick fireplace, wearing soiled jeans and a shirt smudged with something unidentifiable. She claimed that the *Cervantes II,* was Bogart's first boat, but my money was on John Ford.

I looked at her sun-ripened face and knew she could be "as mad as a bee with a bear up its nose," which was something else Lex used to say—especially when she'd been drinking. Lex was contrary enough on a normal day, but when she'd had a couple of shots in her—she preferred Jameson Irish Whiskey—there was no way you could stand near her and not get something on you. Today, I happened to be standing a mite too close.

She was here to help repair one of the twin 185-HP marine engines on the cruiser that I'd been living on for the last year.

"I'm telling you, you're just not cut out for this detective business and you're gonna get hurt, big time." She accepted the sack of fast food and started to chow down on the chicken. I unwrapped a cheeseburger so full of mayo, tomato, and lettuce that it almost slipped out of my hands and onto the deck.

Lex wiggled fingers covered with two kinds of grease—one from the boat's engine and the other from the chicken. "What? No napkins?"

I looked in the bottom of the sack. "Sorry. They must have forgotten."

She seemed to gargle and then went back to the same old song. "Look, honey, I know that you try hard and wanna prove yourself, but it's been almost two years now and look where you are, working out of the back of a rundown restaurant and sleeping nights on this creaky hole in the water."

"The Derby is *not* rundown," I countered, chewing. "It's just seen better times. Like all of us, right? And I sleep on this boat, because the sea breeze clears my sinuses."

She wasn't buying it. She never did. She flipped the lid on an ice chest, reached in, and brought out two cans of Coors. "Yeah, the Brown Derby has seen better days. And so has the agency, if you wanna call it that." She handed over a dripping can of beer.

"Yeah, but success is relative," I said. "You can measure it lots of ways. Mr. P wasn't much of an outward success, but he had a lot of big cases and clients in his day before retiring. People like John Wayne, Peter Lorre, and Joe Lewis."

"I guess. The chief held it together for years before heading to Hawaii and handing things over to you. The problem is, you haven't advanced with the times."

She had a point and knew it. Nowadays, there were plenty of slick, high-class agencies in the yellow pages. Ten of them for every detective show on TV. I thought of one that both Lex and I had known, Johnny Sunset, the ivy-league PI, who had a fast car, a high-rise office and secretary, and a Malibu beach house. Everything, except an eye-patch—the pirate.

He'd won my best girl away from me and wound up marrying her. Then he vanished. I couldn't operate like that. A lot of dazzle and then you're gone, like a photographer's flashbulb. Not my style.

I found myself staring at a funny-looking ring on the top of the Coors can. "What's this thing?"

Lex looked over and saw my confusion. "It's a new way of open the can. Pull the ring and it pops open. Watch." Somehow she yanked at the pull-ring and her can opened with a satisfying snick.

I set my burger aside, fished a finger under the ring of my can and pulled. The ring came off in my hand without opening the can. "Great idea. Now toss me your church key."

Lex shrugged out an opener on a thin chain from around her neck and swung it to me. I popped the top of my beer in the usual manner and squirted foam in my face. Lex howled in delight. "Shit fire and save matches!"

She'd acquired her gravel-pit voice years ago from a chop to the throat in a bar fight. Lex had been in several bar fights. Both her nose and her ears were a little enlarged and flat.

But she had one feature that redeemed all this. She grinned so lopsidedly when she laughed that it made you smile back before you could stop.

"Well, I've got news for you." I wiped my chin. "I picked up a new assignment today, working for NASA."

"What's a NASA?"

I tried to recall what Norman had told me and swore to myself. I needed to start writing these things down in a notepad. The best I could recall was, "The National Air and Space, uh, Academy."

Lex didn't question it. She finished eating. "You know what your trouble is, squirrel? You think too damn much. You need to go on what your gut tells you and not keep backing up and giving people tons of details about where, when, and why stuff happened."

I decided not to argue, for the moment.

Having finished dinner, we started work on the failing engine. Lex loosed a couple of bolts and set them aside. I helped her pull out the fuel pump for inspection, feeling the need to explain. "As to my attention to details, it's an important part of any investigation. Comes from when I started out in the business. Mr. P made me write all those detailed reports."

She smeared her greasy mitts on an equally greasy rag. "See? Ya just did it again."

I frowned.

Lex laughed. "Don't listen to me. I'm just going through a bitter period."

I chocked on my beer and her comment.

She laughed some more and I joined in. We worked on the engine until around two a.m., finally determining that the main problem was a hairline split in a fuel line. During the entire operation, Walt hovered in the back of my mind. Why in the world was he involved with the US Air Force? And what was his "heavy investment" in our county's space program?

CHAPTER 3

Wednesday morning, the clamorous unwinding of the alarm clock tore into my dreams of riding the range on a palomino. I wanted to be a Montana cowboy when I was a kid, but it didn't pan out. So I discovered a different way to fight for justice on the lone frontier.

Stumbling out of my cramped bunk on the cabin cruiser, I took a bucket shower and shaved in the forward head while listening to the radio. There was good news and bad. Residents of Santa Monica were in an uproar over a supposed land grab for beachfront property near the newly opened Pacific Ocean Park. Don Drysdale had pitched for the LA Dodgers and blanked the Phillies one to nothing. Mickey Cohen had taken the fifth again in a senate racket probe in DC. *Life Magazine* was revealing the inside details of the Soviet Secret Police.

I spooned down a bowl of Wheaties with milk from a half-empty quart bottle I'd found in the ice chest. The back of the cereal box told me I could send away for a six-foot, color poster of the Lone Ranger. Tempting, but where would I hang it?

I finished dressing in a new shirt, old tie, and the same sport coat as yesterday. Then I strapped on the beat-up shoulder holster that I'd bought last month at the USA Pawn Shop, locked up the teak and mahogany wheelhouse, and climbed into my trusty Kaiser four-door. Hi-yo silver.

Navigating the surface streets and following Route 66 until it crossed with 99, south of Glendale, I settled back into the long drive north to the Central Valley. I hated traffic. It wasn't heavy today on San Fernando Blvd. but the humidity sure was. The sun scorched the canvas tops of a continuous parade of slow-moving produce trucks. I had to steer around on my way through Sylmar on the new section of the Golden State Freeway. After a few minutes, I turned northwest onto the old faithful Route 14 that wound its way between the San Gabriel Mountains.

It was a long drive, even for Southern California, where everything was so strung out that you needed to pack a lunch to go almost anywhere. I had the twisty two-lane road to myself, for the most part, but the turns in the shadows of the forested hills brought unpleasant thoughts. My mom and dad had crashed their hulking Plymouth on a switchback road like this up in Cold Water Canyon one night back in 1949. At the time, I was playing football and supposedly studying Business Admin at USC. The Highway Patrol found me in the campus library, cramming for a statistics test with a blonde co-ed. The next day, I had to identify the bodies of my parents in the basement of the Beverly Hills hospital.

The CHP never determined exactly why my folks had gone off the road and into a canyon. Deer in the headlights, they said. I'd always thought that that phrase referred to an animal that had frozen, but a young patrolman who had caught the call and later brought me to the chilled basement told me that sometimes it's the driver who freezes.

Despite today's eight-four-degree temperature, I shivered at the memory and switched on the radio, following route 14 into Palmdale. I listened to a steady stream of songs and used-car-lot commercials on KFWB Channel 98 AM "America's number-one Music Station."

Frankie Avalon sang "Venus" and the Platters crooned that "Smoke Gets in Your Eyes." There was something about pink shoelaces, but by that time I'd lost interest.

The landscape flattened as I checked my watch, frowning. It had been over an hour and a half since I'd left the lagoon and I figured that I still had thirty or so miles to go before reaching Edwards Air Force Base. Pulling into a Skelly Oil station for a fill up and a Pepsi, I asked the wrinkle-faced attendant washing my windshield with a spray bottle and squeegee, if this was the right road.

"Sure is, bub." The geezer spat tobacco at a lizard and moved his false teeth around with his tongue. "Just keep on-a going down the Sierra Highway through Palmdale and Lancaster and you can't miss it. Just about all the folks around here work for Uncle Sam's Wind Force, one way or 'nother."

I thanked him, paid, and got back on the road. Sure enough, on the other side of Lancaster, I saw my first road sign for *Edwards AFB*.

I didn't know much about the air base, but I knew a lot about the air force. My brother, Josh, had been in the Army Air Corps and gone down in a fighter plane during the Battle of Midway. I had idolized Josh. For a time, I'd had wanted to be a flyer like him, when I was old enough. I still wore his Bulova aviator's watch. The leather band had long since worn away and I'd replaced it with a stainless steel Twist-O-Flex that all the ads said you could tie in a knot. I liked the band, because I could slip it on my wrist without buckling anything.

The windows were cranked down on the Kaiser and the hot, dry air ruffled my shirt. I positioned my left elbow on the window frame so the air blew up my sleeve and cooled my arm. The road was a gray streak that rippled with the heat through the flat, bleached sands. An infinite line of telephone poles lead me to South Muroc Drive and the entrance to the air base.

Three trailers and a dozen cars were parked along the side of the road near the ten-foot-high chain-link fence and concrete guardhouse. A crowd of civilians milled around outside the red and white toll arm that spanned the entrance drive. My arrival galvanized the crowd. They saw me and grabbed placards that read *Peace* and others that read *Dis-Armament Now*. One of the signs was a stick drawling of a chicken's foot inside a circle. I thought I recognized a few faces among the protestors.

A man with a wet bandana plastered to the top of his skull came around my side of the car. "Sir, we hope that you are not going in there."

I smiled. "I sort of planned on it."

"We would urge you not to," shouted a young woman in enormous sunglasses.

A young, goateed man stepped forward. "Do you know what they have in there?"

Before I could answer, "Airplanes?" his mouth twisted and he said loudly, "Bombs and guns and gas!"

A couple of the members of the crowd took up the chant: "Bombs and guns and gas. Bombs and guns and gas." Some of them were marching now, knees pumping, and wielding their placards. A guard looked out the window of his brick building and spoke to someone on a phone.

I, too, raised my voice. "Sorry, folks. I'm going in. I'd appreciate it if you'd step aside."

Surprisingly, the chant ended and they lowered their signs. I put the car in gear and slowly pulled up to the guard station.

There were two uniformed men in the building and I showed one of them my California driver's license and the letter from Walt. The other guard stayed on the phone, but nodded to his buddy. My guard brought his rifle up in a half salute. "You're expected, sir," he snapped.

I put away my credentials and gestured at the firearm. "Is that thing loaded?"

He brought it down and became more casual. "We're not packing live ammo, sir. It's a precaution to avoid any accidents with those annoying peace-niks."

I nodded knowingly and asked where the security office was.

"Just follow the sergeant and he'll take you Colonel Scott."

An air force three-striper jumped into a jeep and we proceeded past several rows of non-descript, one-story buildings that I took to be enlisted men's barracks, machine shops, and storage sheds.

Under the dragon-roar of a jet engine warming up nearby, we steered between open hangers as big as Utah, finally coming to a stop in a small parking lot in front of a wide, flat windowless structure labeled *Building E* and in smaller letters *Air Force High-Speed Flight Test Center*.

Inside, a guard at a reception counter had me patted down and took my .38 revolver. "You won't need this, sir." He shook the cartridges into his palm. "You can pick it up when you leave."

"Can I get a receipt?"

He looked at the gun like it was a dead frog. "For this old thing? Negative, sir." His military manner was brisk. "But I'll lock it in the safe. Come along."

We half-step marched past metal desks, filing cabinets, and clacking typewriters. I was summarily dispatched into the office of the Chief Security Officer, Colonel Fielding Scott.

A blocky blond man in a summer-weight uniform came out from between a worn wooden desk and a wide, louvered window to shake my hand and call over my shoulder, "Hold my calls, Sergeant."

There was a clipped "Yes, sir" and the sound of the door closing behind me, as Scott introduced himself and offered me a chair. An air conditioner hummed in the window.

While he went back behind his desk, where a photo of his wife and daughter sat in a silver frame, I glanced around. The office walls displayed a map of the entire base, a few framed citations, and a row of aerial photos of jet planes. There was a blue F-86 Sabre, a black X-15, and an orange XS-1. Colorful career.

The colonel unfolded a leather pouch and began stuffing tobacco into a well-chewed pipe. Then he opened up on me with both barrels. "I don't mind telling you, Mr. Wade, that I'm against your being here. But the base commander ordered me to engage with you, even though my department has already conducted a full investigation and concluded that Captain Taffe's death was an accident. Seems that NASA and other higher ups want an objective SitRep, even though we've had deaths here on the base in the past."

"Usually," I countered, "those deaths were from obvious crashes or happened in front of witnesses, right?"

He clamped down on the stem of his pipe and looked straight at me. "Usually," he allowed. "I don't know how much you know about our operations, so why don't you level the playing field and fill me in?"

Nice strategy, pushing it back on me. I took a breath and shot a load of Norman at him. "I know that Edwards has been the home of air speed testing since World War II. And, that Project Mercury will test and select its astronauts for operations from this base. That means you are all under a microscope here and can't afford a screw up, because the nation needs this affair wrapped up yesterday, since the Soviets are kicking our butts in space."

As if on cue, the room shook from an overhead sonic boom. I waited for the windows to stop rattling and the colonel to get his pipe going.

"I also know that NASA is a civilian agency and that

the military has to operate under their non-military supervision."

Scott scowled and blew smoke. "The charter of our mission is for peaceful purposes for the benefit of all mankind."

"Yes, I like Ike, too. And I've always slept better at night, knowing that you guys are on the job."

"You're damn right."

He was getting as hot as the Mojave. I decided to try and defuse the situation. "All of which, is mere background for why I'm here. You've got a dead pilot, whom I'm betting was one of your leading candidates for astronaut school."

A box on Colonel Scott's desk buzzed. A tinny voice said, "Sir? Major Kirkman is here as you requested."

Scott poked the box and growled. "Send him in."

I rose from my chair and watched a lean man enter the office and close the door. He was about six feet, an inch taller than me, but he looked like a runner, which made him appear shorter. We shared the same colored hair and eyes—brown. His grip was strong and his voice was richly confident. "Roger Kirkman, Base Information Officer and Public Relations Liaison with NASA for Project Mercury."

With his mustache and natural elegance, he reminded me of Smilin' Jack. I grinned at the thought and he grinned back.

I fished out a business card. It still had my old address on it, but I handed it over anyway. "Stan Wade, professional investigations."

He looked at the card and then back at me, a bit confused. "I think I've heard that name before."

I showed him my full grill. "I get that a lot."

He came farther into the room and we all sat down.

"So, what has the colonel already told you?"

"Not much. I've been doing all the talking."

Scott leaned back. "I've been waiting for you, Major, to fill Mr. Wade in."

"Yes sir, sir." Kirkman turned to me. "As you may know, the base has a long-standing successful relationship with the movie and television industries. An unnamed representative, from the team who has been involved in filming the Steve Canyon TV series here, has suggested that you be given a free hand in reviewing our investigation."

"That, gentlemen, is exactly why I'm here. So tell me where's the body?"

Kirkman shot a glance at the colonel, who said, "We'll take you to it."

CHAPTER 4

The three of us climbed into a red-hot jeep and Kirkman drove us over blazing concrete, past the base movie theater where the marquee said they were showing *North by Northwest*. The military certainly got special treatment from Hollywood. We didn't even have that one down in LA yet.

We turned a corner and parked in the shade of a shoebox shaped small building that turned out to be the base morgue. I relished the air conditioning inside, but didn't care at all for the alcoholic miasma with chloroform or formaldehyde.

Somewhere a faucet dripped, and while I put on a cloth face mask and shoved my hands into powered, rubber gloves, a couple of lab-coated attendants stood by as we uncovered the slanted, stone table where lay the naked body of Arthur Taffe, ex-captain of the United States Air Force.

I'd seen dead bodies in morgues before. All of them naked. All of them dead. You would think that, over time, I'd have picked up on some of the technical aspects and jargon, but whenever I looked at a dead body in a morgue, all I could see was a dead body. His half-opened eyes would never see outer space. Or maybe that's what they were seeing now.

Kirkman spoke through his mask. "The white foam residue around his mouth and nostrils is from dried mucus and confirms that Captain Taffe was breathing when he entered the pool."

"If he was breathing," I said, "then he might have been awake. So how did he drown?"

"We believe that he slipped, hit his head, and fell in the water," Scott answered.

Taffe's body lay before us trim and pale, but I could see tan lines where he'd worn his shorts, watch, and ring.

"Was he nude, like this when he was found?"

"No." Kirkman coughed slightly. "He was wearing a high-altitude-flight test suit. We took the liberty of removing it in order to perform a preliminary autopsy. We've sent blood and tissue samples to the lab for testing of foreign substances. It's standard procedure."

"I see." I backed away into a wheeled table and caused a stainless steel pan to bounce off the tiled floor with a diminishing series of clangs. "Ah, let's go to the scene of the—let's go to the pool where he died."

We got out of our lab gear and back into the jeep. Hot, clammy minutes later, we were inside a huge, echoing hanger-sized enclosure filled with exercise equipment and strange devices used for testing pilot's physical endurance. Basically, it was a glorified gym, complete with a thirty-by-sixty-foot swimming pool.

Kirkman pointed into the water. "The body was found here at 0600 hours by Technical Sergeant Bud Clarke, who maintains the pool. The area was immediately secured."

I gazed around and saw two entrances to the enormous room. The pair of double doors that we'd come in through and, off in the distance, a roll-up overhead door presumably connected to a loading dock. I got out a pad and ballpoint pen and started taking notes.

"We think that he drown sometime in the night after 2000 hours," Colonel Scott explained. "Taffe had been scheduled to test the buoyancy compensation in a new flight suit the next morning."

"All of our astronaut candidates are gung ho and detail-oriented," Major Kirkman volunteered. "He was probably checking out the suit for himself, when he slipped, unfortunately."

Scott pointed up to a small device in the rafters above our heads. "We'll know for certain once the film comes back from the lab."

I studied the high ceiling. "Impressive security, Colonel."

"Maybe," he grunted. "It's out of my hands. The powers that be want the sixteen-mm film developed off site. Part of the 'objective investigation,' like you."

We moved on to the building's locker room, where I met Sergeant Bud Clarke, who forced the lock on Taffe's locker. Clarke was a "twenty-year man" who was marking time toward his retirement. He had doughy features, thinning hair, and a paunch. I questioned him about finding the body, but didn't learn anything new.

Inside Taffe's locker, we found his semi-dress uniform—light-blue dress shirt, dark-blue trousers with his cover still tucked into the web belt. Black, polished shoes. Sunglasses in a clam-like case. Keys, Camels, and a Zippo. Comb, handkerchief, wristwatch, loose change, dog tags, and an open pack of Dentyne gum. In his wallet were thirty-six dollars, his air force ID, driver's license, and a photo of a good-looking dark-haired young lady.

"Any idea who she is?" I asked.

Kirkman shook his head.

"Don't know her name," Scott said. "But I met her with Captain Taffe a few weeks ago at a social gathering in Hollywood."

"Social gathering?" I waved the photo at Scott. "Mind if I use this to try and find out who she is?"

Kirkman started to protest, but Scott said, "We'll make a photo copy of it first at my office."

I tucked the photo into my shirt pocket, as we walked to the jeep.

On the way back, I took a page from Lex's book and followed my gut. "I don't think it was an accident, gentlemen. It's too convenient that he slipped and died all alone at night."

"For the good of the project, we should investigate fully," Scott shouted over the roar of a nearby jet.

"Taffe was a bit of a loner," Kirkman agreed, adding, "but I really doubt that he'd—I doubt that it's a homicide." He went on to say that he thought perhaps the protestors should be investigated, but with a low profile. "We're already fighting on several fronts to maintain a positive image. We have enough problems. For instance, that letter from a girl back east, Hillary Rodham, who wants to be an astronaut and keeps sending letters asking why there are no women candidates. People just don't understand the importance of this program." I must have given him the fish eye, because he said, "Don't look at me like that. America needs experienced, aeronautical engineering test pilots to ensure total success and that means men. There are no women test pilots, thus no women astronauts."

Scott seemed to not be listening. "You know?" he said. "There might be something to the protestor idea, but I don't see how any of them could have gotten past security and onto the base."

"I've heard that the Reliance Management Corporation could arrange for the protests to end," Kirkman said.

The roar of the jets quieted temporarily, so I decided to join the conversation. "What is the Reliance Management Corporation?"

"They operate a fleet of trucks that handle the waste management on the base," Kirkman explained.

"Sounds like the Mob. Maybe I'll check into them."

"Colonel Scott can get you their address and have someone set up a meeting there later this afternoon."

Back at Building E, we climbed out of the jeep.

"We just need this thing to end ASAP," Scott said.

"But keep things discreet, Mr. Wade," Kirkman advised. "Don't forget that these astronauts are national heroes. They're clean-cut, all-American boys, ready for single combat versus worldwide communism."

Major Kirkman was typical of every PR man I'd ever met, worried about image over everything else.

☙❦❧

Twenty minutes later, I collected my .38 and pocketful of rounds and drove back to the air base's main gate. There were fewer picketers outside the fence than before. I didn't blame them. It had been a hot day and many of them looked frazzled.

When they saw me coming, they gathered their forces and brought forward their most recognizable members. I'd heard that Greg Peck and Tony Perkins were outspoken on disarmament, but couldn't believe I was seeing them approach.

Both men wore ball caps and loose, dusty clothing. Their faces glistened with perspiration.

Peck approached my car and showed his open palm. "We've got something here that we'd like you to read," he said in a resonating voice.

"Surprised to see you here," I told him. "Someone told me that you were over at MGM, shooting a war movie."

He gave me a pained expression. "Actually, *Pork Chop Hill* is an *anti*-war movie. We all do what we can, when we can."

Perkins reached into a canvas bag and handed him a sheet of paper. "You'll understand better after you read this."

The guy with the beatnik goatee, that I'd noticed before, edged toward our conversation. "That'll change your mind about a lot of things," he said.

Peck handed over the paper. It was a printed flyer that appeared to reproduce an article from the *Los Angeles Times* concerning "arms proliferation." General Curtis Lamay was quoted as saying that the US had 1000 bombers with nuclear weapons, in case of a world crisis.

I looked at Perkins. "And you're supposed to be working with Hitchcock on a TV psycho movie."

Perkins tilted his head and smiled. "You're very well informed, Mr…"

"Stan Wade," I told them. "Investigator. I read the trades. It's how I get my best clients."

Peck gave me a suspicious look. "Seems like I've heard that name somewhere before."

"Yeah, well…look, guys, I admire what you're doing here, but—"

Out of a clear sky, another sonic boom thundered over our heads and we all flinched.

Goatee's eyes lit up and he grabbed hold of the open car window frame. "They've got chemical weapons in there, man. It's a wild scene," he said with a slight accent. "They store tabun in tanks on that base. Gas and bombs and guns." His eyes were intense.

Peck and Perkins urged him back. "Just read it, okay?" Perkins said. "The doomsday clock is ticking. This country and the whole world need to disarm before it's too late."

I wedged the paper under my right thigh on the car seat. Perkins's eyes were intense, too. "Thanks. I'll be sure to give it a good read."

As I nudged the gas pedal and moved the Kaiser slowly away, Peck raised his palm again, just like Dave Garroway. "Peace."

CHAPTER 5

During the long drive back to LA, I thought about a lot of things. I thought about what I'd seen of Taffe's body, his effects, and the supposed scene of his death. I thought of the peace-nik protestors and whether or not they had a motive or the ability to be involved in Taffe's death. And I thought that I was being followed.

I had stopped off at Sam's of San Fernando for a late lunch and was just leaving the gravel parking lot when I saw in the rearview mirror that I'd picked up a tail. It was a dark blue Chevy with white sidewall tires and an adjustable spotlight mounted in front of the driver's door.

It followed for quite a while from a safe distance. Then, as I drove back into the city and neared the Hughes

Aircraft plant, it peeled off into a side street, as if it had given up the chase. I steered north on McConnell Avenue, over the fetid Ballona Creek, and arrived at the six-story headquarters of the Reliance Management Corporation.

Walking up the stone steps and in the main entrance to the elevators, I thought I passed a guy with a heads-down, intense expression that I could have sworn was Jimmy Hoffa. The Teamsters had been getting a lot of press lately and none of it positive.

The elevator quietly played an orchestral version of "True Love" and lifted me to the top of the building. There was a row of ceiling-to-floor windows looking out at the far Pacific and a corner office, where I presented another of my dwindling supply of business cards to E. Irwin Worthmyer, President of Reliance Management. I wondered what the "E" stood for.

Worthmyer was tall, trim with gray hair and mustache—almost like something from central casting for a corporate president. He came forward to meet me in the middle of an office big enough to bowl in. The room contained a desk the size of two Ping-Pong tables and a chair with a back taller than I was. Filling out the office were three full couches, half a dozen client chairs, and a board-room table for twenty. A lot of splash-and-smear art hung on the walls, as well as framed color photos of Worth-myer shaking mitts with the chief of police, the LA County Sheriff, and even Jack Webb.

E. Irwin wasn't the only person in the room. Apparently, he'd planned to conduct a staff meeting while we met, since various VPs and office workers came and went while we chatted and he answered phones. At this pace, I figured him for a coronary any minute.

"I have no idea why Colonel Scott sent you to me, Mr. Wade." His tanned smile failed to disguise the diamond-tipped drill of his gray eyes. He kept his posture erect, his face stern, and his manner brisk, despite his red and green bow tie and the background conversations and ringing phones. In turn, I kept him busy long enough that others in the room started taking his calls.

We talked for all of ten minutes in that airport-terminal environment. I got almost nothing out of the man. And he got almost nothing out of me. He tried to hire me. I told him that I already had a client. He wondered who it was. I wondered why he wanted to know. He didn't like that. I didn't like him. But I was surprised to see that I recognized one of the women who stepped behind his desk to answer his phones.

She was a slim redhead, who filled out a pink blouse and skirt nicely and wore heels and dainty white gloves. *In the office?* She caught my eye while straightening the phone cord and looked cross while minutely shaking her head at me.

I hadn't seen Suzi in two years, ever since her husband had left her, but she and I went back a long way. I'd last seen her and Johnny when I was checking invitations at a swank party given by Eddie and Debbie at the Beverly Hills Hotel. I'd heard that she'd closed up Sunset Investigations after he'd gone, but why was she here now, doing secretarial work, and why was she giving me that frown?

Worthmyer consented that Reliance held the contracts for waste management at Edwards and that he'd be happy to do whatever was necessary to secure a similar agreement with the base for the continued construction and expansion there. He was indeed concerned about the potential threat posed by the peace-niks and that "America's defense against the Russians must be firm, complete, and absolute."

The beehive buzz around E. Irwin and me seemed to pause when he said that. I got the idea that the protestors would be gone tomorrow, if the government would sign new contracts with Reliance today.

I could see that I was dealing with a closed mind and decided to take some air before everybody in the room broke into a chorus of "God Bless America." It was time to go and I said so.

Worthmyer patted my shoulder and shook my hand at the same time. "Pleased to have met you, Mr. Wade. Pass my comments along to your contacts at the air base, won't you?"

I assured him I would and took one last glance at Suzi as I was walking out. She mouthed the word "later" to me from behind a file folder.

❧❧❧

I remembered the scene from *Casablanca* where Bogart waited nearly all night for Ingrid Bergman at Rick's Café. It wasn't all that late this evening at the Brown Derby, but patrons were starting to thin out during the brief gap between dinner and the return of the post-theatre crowd.

I thought about Suzi and Johnny and how he had disappeared. I recalled that she had suspected that the Mob was involved, somehow, but she hadn't been able to prove anything. I had offered to help, but she was determined to do it herself. She'd always been fiery like that, but when had she become a redhead?

Sunset Investigations had been a competing firm that had risen rapidly to success in the LA basin. Where I had stumbled along in a one-man agency, Johnny Sunset, whose real name was Segundo, had flourished with his fancy TV looks and high-class clients. He dressed swell, had a $10 haircut, foreign sports car, and always got the girl, including, eventually, Suzi.

I'd known her back when we were in our teens and once had shared bubble gum. We had met over summer vacation at a dude ranch that our parents had individually sent us to and she had cleaned me out of cat-eyes, steelies, milkies, and clearies. She was a terror then and a heartbreaker soon after.

Back then, however, I was far from home and lost,

literally. One summer in 1946, I'd gone over the hill to "light out for the territory" and gotten completely turned around. I spent the night alone somewhere in Placerita Canyon while spraining an ankle and nearly catching pneumonia before the search team from the Rough and Ready Ranch found me.

Ironically, I suddenly realized that I had passed near the same location twice today while driving east of Santa Clarita on my way to and from Edwards.

Now here I was, finishing a plate of spaghetti and working on my fourth cigarette, when she came in.

She cast a glance around the room, brushed past the métier d', and then came straight at me, speaking the pet name she'd given me when we were kids. "Standy."

I stood up, looked in her soft blue eyes, and saw the worry line between them.

CHAPTER 6

I found myself staring and a little dizzy. Maybe I'd gotten up too fast.

The name Standy was a playful combination of my first name and middle initial. I'd known this engaging woman back when she was Suzanne Evans and we were both confused teenagers. In fact, I'd known her longer than anyone else still kicking around Southern California.

I said one word, "Suzi."

"Are you going to ask me to sit down?"

"Yes, of course. Please." I scooched around in the booth and she slid in next to me. Chanel No. 5. "It's good to see you," I said. "Been a couple of years and I wasn't sure that it was you in that red wig."

Her platinum hair was brushed back in a Toni perm,

like June Allyson's. She adjusted a stray bang on her forehead and leaned in to me for an air kiss. "I would have called you months ago, but I've been keeping a low profile."

I supposed that my next move should have been to talk business, but now she was reaching over and touching the white streak in my hair.

"This is new," she said.

My face felt warm. "It's my curse," I said. "I got it in a knife fight."

Her blue eyes sparkled. "Let me guess. You were outside Griffith Observatory with James Dean's ghost?"

I tried to concentrate. "Something like that."

"What then?"

A waiter in a mess jacket came over, saw that it was me, and turned to leave.

"Ah, Gus?" I called after him. "A couple of Bacardi and Cokes, please."

He turned, nodded, and went away.

I let out a breath and stumbled on. "I got it stopping a guy up in Bel Air, who attempted to confront Bing Crosby during the filming of *High Society*." As soon as I'd said it, I realized how preposterous it sounded, even for Hollywood.

The blue sparkle widened. "Seriously?"

I held my breath for a beat. "Actually, I cut myself shaving."

Her laugh was like musical, Chinese bells.

Gus came back with our drinks and we toasted grandly.

Vincent Price was at a corner table arguing with the chief. Suddenly, Price roared back in laughter and slapped the chief on the back. The two men were pals again.

"So what were you doing at Reliance Management?" Suzi asked.

I was relieved at the change of subject. "I'm working a case that involves them—possibly. What are you doing there and why the red wig and gloves, even?"

She was prepared for the question. "I'm on a case, too. The big one."

"About Johnny?"

She nodded and took a sip of her drink. "I'm working with the LAPD to get information on Reliance and its connection to the Mob."

I straightened. "Undercover for the cops and wearing gloves to avoid fingerprints. God, Suzi. Are you nuts?"

"No. Mickey and the Mob are behind Johnny's disappearance. I'm sure of it." She fiddled with the ring on her left hand. "That bastard Cohen actually put out odds that Johnny would never be found."

Just about everybody in town knew Mickey Cohen, our neat, short, west-coast racketeer. And everyone knew you could get a bet down on just about anything with his gang of bookies. Trouble was that lately he ran a tight organization and had always found a way to get out of any indictment. I recalled hearing that he was currently in Washington DC, being grilled by some senator, named Kennedy. So, Suzi was safe, sort of, until the creep returned.

I tried to find out more. "So, Worthmyer is connected?"

"Actually," she said, "as far as I've been able to tell, he knows nothing, but is shielded by attorneys, accountants, and Mob-placed VPs."

"His first initial is 'E.' Does that stand for Edgar or Edward?"

"More like Ego."

Donald O'Conner came in the Derby's front entrance and started to be seated in a booth across the aisle. He caught sight of me and quickly dashed out without ordering. The poor guy was between films. He had run up a heavyweight tab here and knew that I knew it.

"Suzi, I don't think you should be messing around with these guys. I'm not even sure you should be messing around with the LAPD."

She put her hand on my arm. "I'm just taking a page out of your book, Standy. Ever since I've known you, you've been a loner and wanted to be a private eye. Now it's my turn. And for a damn good reason."

I felt my throat tighten. "And ever since I've known you, you've wanted to be like Simon Templar and rob the robbers. Suzi, that's not real. You could get killed."

I sat there a minute and stared into her earnest eyes,

but it became too much, so I glanced away. "Let me help you."

I heard her sigh. "Like you said, Standy, it's dangerous and you don't know what you're walking into."

"But you could tell me," I said. "I know you need this and I want to help."

We talked for a bit more, but I gently urged her to see things from my point of view. She told me her suspicions, which were too general to prove anything, and I could see that if I didn't step in, she would eventually stumble and fall into something well over her head.

We talked for almost an hour, and the rest of the world seemed to fade. I promised to be careful and she thanked me with proper reserve. We parted as the after-dinner crowd filled the booths around us. I walked her to her Fairlane, where we kissed briefly, before she pulled out onto Welshire and was gone.

I knew that I'd committed myself to swim into deep waters now and, if I wasn't going to drown, I'd need all of my skill, plus a little extra protective gear.

☙❧

I had learned long ago from my mentor that every time it rained, it rained…rain. And that the best offence was…an offence. Barring that, the second best offence was a defense, which was why I regretfully parted from Suzi and took my Kaiser to see Norman.

When he wasn't constructing his zombie novel or reading science fiction, Norman was constructing something from science fact. Last year, he worked for almost a month, building a piece of hardware that needed something he called "software," which I could use to look up the address and phone number of anyone in the LA phone book. When I pointed out that I could do the very same thing by simply using the actual phone book, he was undaunted. "You'll see, Mr. Wade. Just wait."

On the other hand, Norman was a whiz at photography, developing my worst exposures taken in the worst light, even when I was on the run, making them come out like something shot by James Wong Howe. Plus, he had a knack for turning things like those little Japanese radios into listening and transmitting devices that came in handy during stakeouts.

The only real regret I had was that Norman imagined too much and tended to be paranoid. He often told me that the government was out to spy on us all, in order to defend against communism. I was pretty sure that his favorite TV show was *I Led 3 Lives*. However, he was a good friend and worth the trouble. I always got more from him than I bargained for—good and bad.

This evening, I pulled up to the TV repair shop where he worked, even though it was after closing time, because I'd learned that Norman would be working on something he called a "facts" machine.

He answered the door, let me in, and proceeded to

demonstrate. "And the reasonable facsimile of the document comes out here, exactly like the original," he explained, shoving his glasses back up the bridge of his thin nose. He pulled a sheet of paper out of his machine and waved it right before my eyes. And the printing on the sheet blurred from the movement into a smear right before my eyes.

He seemed disappointed, but only for a heartbeat. "Ah, don't worry. I just have to tone up the heating element and it'll work like nobody's business."

"I believe you, Norm," I offered. "It'll be great for everybody's business someday, but right now I need you to finish installing that auto-radio thing in my car. Can you do that?"

"The portable car-phone?" He almost scratched his ear with a screwdriver. "Well, I haven't worked all the bugs out of it yet. I got distracted by Vampira on *Shock Theater* the other night and started work on a blood analysis system that could help identify people better than fingerprints."

Over the next hour, I kept directing the conversation back to where I needed it and eventually he was handing me the telephone receiver that now connected to my dashboard between the car's radio and the steering column.

"You can answer calls by pressing this," he said, pointing to a square, red button on the inside surface of the receiver. "But to make a call out, you just have to spin the dial here on the dash, which I don't recommend that you do while driving. It's too much of a distraction to the right lobe of your brain and if you're going thirty miles per hour, you'll travel a distance of over fifteen yards before—"

"Okay, Norm. I got it. I won't drink, or dial, and drive."

"Good." He beamed. "You ever heard of Forest J. Ackerman?"

"No, does he have one of these auto-phones, too?"

"No, but Elvis Presley does. Ackerman has this new magazine with pictures of movie monsters and Vampira. She's going to be in a movie herself pretty soon. Something about corpses invaded by Martians."

"No kidding? Sounds interesting, Norm, but I need to know if this phone thing is safe. You put a bank of batteries for it in my trunk. It won't blow up the car or shock me or anything, will it?"

Judging from Norman's reactions, this seemed to be the looniest thing I'd said all night.

"The worst thing about the system," he said, through his laughter, "is that you'll get a lot of static, but not the kind that shocks you. It's the kind that you hear over the phone. Like *buzsptik*. That, and it might drop reception when you go through a tunnel or under a high-tension wire, or too fast down a steep hill, or—"

"Okay, Norm. That sounds swell. Thanks. This will help me a lot. I'm grateful you let me borrow it—"

"Test it," he corrected me. We were getting into overlapping dialogue. "Beta testing is why I'm letting you use it."

"Right," I agreed. "I'm beta testing it for you. And I promise to report back regularly, so you can tell how well it's working and improve it."

"Correct," he said. "In the meantime, you should call me at the base phone exchange number a couple of times a day, so I can record the system's function. I think Ackerman would be a great agent for my novel. He represents a lot of science fiction guys. Calls them sci-fi writers."

"Good, Norman. That's good and good night."

On the way back to Santa Monica and the cabin cruiser, I tried to make a call on the phone, but all I got was fuzzy noise and crackling static. Maybe it was because I was driving past the gala lights of the new *Al Capone* movie premiere, at the time. I decided to try it again in the morning.

CHAPTER 7

At 7 a.m., I was going through my morning routine again. Stretch, shave, brush teeth and hair, dress. I noticed that the Wheaties box was almost empty. Had the boat been burgled during the night, or had I just lost track of details again? I got out my notebook and wrote down *grocery*, but I still felt uneasy. Maybe it was because today I planned to meet with some very unfriendly people.

When I started out in this business, I would have given my back teeth for a chance to go up against organized crime. Now, I wasn't so eager.

In my early years, it was all about heroics and proving myself. I wanted to right wrongs and battle evil, just like in the comics and detective stories. Since my trick shoulder had kept me out of the army during the Korean conflict, I'd looked for other ways to heroically prove my worth. I'd excelled in the Boy Scouts and tested my endurance playing left tackle for USC, until the shoulder problem. That and my crummy grades got me bounced from college in 1949.

And, since my family died that same year, I knew that I'd hit the muddy bottom and my ideas of being a big hero began to seem like an idiot's tale. I'd had nowhere useful to go—and didn't really want to, for that matter—and then I'd met Mr. P.

He didn't seem like a hero at first, to my muddled thinking. He was old—pushing 60, overweight—pushing 200 pounds, and hung around with Lex—who was the epitome of pushy. But he was the most patient, methodical, and considerate man I'd ever met. He acted like he genuinely wanted other people to get along better than he did. That was a new kind of hero for me. Not dynamic and powerful, but thoughtful, quiet, and clever. He made a success of being a private detective by hanging in and hanging back until the right moment to solve the case.

He'd been doing this for years when I met him. And that was the bad news. I wanted to work with him and, in his usual manner, he didn't complain, which was the good news. He accepted me and taught me the real way to clearly and completely work a case.

I'd started out by fetching Pepsi's and tacos and answering the phone. I took notes and wrote reports and fed his cat. Eventually, he got jammed up and needed help on a stakeout. I spent the night happy to be huddled in a dark doorway in an ally across from the Westwood Motor Inn in April of 1955. I was waiting to catch sight of Mickey Cohen for Ben Hecht.

Cohen had recently come out of prison and Hecht had wanted to find him for research on the screenplay for Otto Preminger's *The Man with the Golden Arm*. Mickey had kept a low profile, until I found him. Nothing important ever came from the meeting, but I got my first taste that night of the success that can come from careful, methodical investigation. From then on, I gave up my ideas of heroic adventure and started acting like a serious detective. I had finally found an identity I could believe in.

That was also the first time I'd crossed paths with Mickey Cohen. And it wouldn't be the last, which was why I'd come prepared for trouble this morning. I had Norman's car phone for extra protection and at least one other trick up my sleeve.

Not that I condoned Mickey in any way or the bloody deaths that just seemed to collect coincidentally around him over the years, but I had to admit that the little creep affected a measure of class. Unlike the other gangsters we'd all read about when we were young—Capone, Nitti, and Dillinger, or even Siegel, Lansky, and Giancana—Mickey flaunted a public persona, eating at elegant restaurants, dressing to a tee, and owning a high-class men's clothing store. He was a new type of mobster—in appearance only—and he loved to show up for a night on the town or an interview with the press. He was a Hollywood hood and I knew that his beauty was as false as an eyelash by *Maybelline.*

Underneath the expensive haircut and cologne lived a mind like a lint trap and a heart of granite. Better than Mr. Lucky, he held the gambling concessions in greater LA in his sweaty palm and fostered a pack of henchmen who were experts in arm twisting and leg breaking. Even now, while Mickey was out of town in DC, the machine he operated continued to grind away at the poor saps that fell into his path.

As I thought about this and drove casually through the short, mean streets of Santa Monica, I caught the national news playing in the background on the car radio. Our current draught was setting a sixty-year record, but a blizzard was ripping through the Midwest. The US had agreed to send thirty missiles to Italy. Eruptions on the sun were blocking international radio communications. Tab Hunter would appear that night on the Pat Boone show.

I switched it off in the middle of Connie Francis singing "My Happiness" and pulled into the one place in town where I knew I could always connect with the Mob. It sounded ridiculous, but Mickey ran an ice cream parlor on Grandville Avenue in Brentwood, among the well-to-do homes and the gracious residential streets. The cute, little shop was situated in a small row of interconnected storefronts in front of a wooded lot. As I pulled into the empty parking lot and set the hand brake on the Kaiser, I saw that a small print shop and a swimming pool supply store shared the building with the ice cream shop. During the drive here, I'd noticed in the rearview mirror that I needed a haircut. I'd also noticed a gray late-model Plymouth sedan. Just before I'd pulled into the parking lot, it had turned off and glided away down the tree-lined road, leaving me to feel like a bug under a magnifying glass. I hoped that I wouldn't get burned by the intense rays.

As I approached the entrance to the ice cream shop, I saw a sign on the door that read, "Closed Thursdays." I knocked anyway, but got no response. I put a hand up to the window to peer in and saw no one.

Damn! There was nobody here.

Hot damn! There's nobody here!

I knocked again and listened to the birds and the wind in the jacaranda trees overhead. Nothing happened.

I looked about. Nothing happening.

I went around behind the buildings to a small alley next to the woods. Nothing there.

I tried the rear entrance of the shop, thinking that the place likely had something to do with Cohen's bookie activities. Naturally, the door was locked, but it gave a little when I leaned my weight on it. I leaned some more—harder—and it gave with a crunch of dried wood.

I waited. Nothing. Who would have thought that "nothing" could be this exciting?

Inside, I saw that the back room contained several large, lift-top freezers for the ice cream and a desk with three phones. There was a small, wood-burning stove filled with ashes from burned papers. Evidence?

There were two doors leading out of the back room. One took me down a short hall that lead into a classic 1980s soda fountain room with tiny tables, chairs, and an overhead fan that was not spinning. The room was dominated by an enormous marble lunch counter backed by a mirror that filled the wall. Nothing and nobody.

I went back to try the second door. This one was behind the desk with the phones and opened easily into the darkened back area of the print shop next door. I stepped in and heard a faint creaking noise in the distance. I froze and automatically reached under my left arm, resting my hand on my shoulder holster. More nothing. I decided that nothing was my best friend.

I scanned around the room and found stacks and reams of paper, cans of ink in various colors, and several hand-operated printing presses, large and table-top models. In a waste basket were wrinkled-up copies of the flyer that reprinted the disarmament story from the *LA Times*. I heard the creaking sound again, beyond another door to my left.

Slowly, I tried the door and found it unlocked. It connected to the third business in the building, the swimming pool supply company. I pressed my luck and crossed the threshold.

It was an industrial storeroom, filled with rows and shelves of chemical supplies and stacks of rubber tubing and plastic hoses. There was a battered, wooden office desk pushed up against a wall. The wall contained a Ridged Tool calendar and a couple of *Playboy* pinups; Miss July and Miss August of last year. The desk contained a locked drawer, which I unlocked with a conveniently located claw hammer. Inside the drawer, I found a pile of wallets and key chains. One of the wallets held a 1956 California driver's license issued to Johnny Sunset.

I thought I heard a car pull up in the parking lot out front, which is what distracted me from the creaking noise behind me. I felt a jarring thump in the back of my skull, as I vowed never to be excited by nothing again. I half turned, but got another, harder hit on the head for my effort. Fireworks went off behind my eyes and slowly faded, falling away into blackness.

CHAPTER 8

When I was a young boy, the "enemy" lived across either of two oceans, plotting our destruction. Then in the early '50s, it had moved to the other side of the planet, ready to attack from on high over the North Pole. Now it was beeping at us from outer space, still ironically growing bigger and deadlier, the farther it moved away.

I couldn't begin to figure it. That's why I kept my feet on the hard earth of home and worked on simple, mundane domestic and urban crimes. Life seemed so much safer that way, except for today.

The gull-wing hood ornament of my Kaiser was sailing along the highway in front of me at an odd angle, while I tried to recall what planet I was on. I was in the passenger seat with a nasty headache. The car was moving along at a fair clip through the evening traffic that streamed north and east. The radio was on. My hands were cramped behind my back by cold metal. I peered left through a half-closed eye, pretending to still be unconscious. It was an Academy Award performance.

A gawky guy was at the wheel. He hadn't shaved in a couple days and the thick, brown hair on the top of his head stuck out in all directions. He wore the work clothes of a maintenance man. The cuffs of his trousers were frayed and every time he shifted his feet, his shoes creaked. The radio reported that California prisons were overcrowded and that Raymond Chandler had died at the Scripps Clinic down in La Jolla. Before I could stop myself, I said, "Dammit."

"Ah, the clubfoot's awake," the driver said, showing me a mouthful of stained teeth. "Don't try anything, or I'll pull over and belt you again."

"I'm not a cop," I said in a dry voice. "I'm private."

"What's that mean?"

I didn't think he understood and I didn't feel like explaining.

"Don't fuck with me," he said, fishing out a Viceroy and punching in the car's cigarette lighter. He gestured with his chin at Norman's car phone. "You got a police radio."

The car lighter would have made a great weapon, if I could've reached it. "Where are we going?"

He lit his filter-tip smoke, puffed, and pushed the lighter back into the dash. "Don't worry, copper. We're almost there." He swung the steering wheel over hard to the left and we pulled onto a two-lane that rose into the hills as the sun was fading. I saw a sign that read "Lost Valley Road" and didn't like what it suggested.

A couple of minutes later, we turned left again and followed a gravel road. The radio was singing, "I had a girl and Donna was her name," when we stopped at a rough-hued ranch house, complete with barn and fenced corral. I didn't see any livestock, but I heard a chicken cluck. There was soft, foggy moonlight, but I was too distracted to think of a simile.

My driver shut off the engine and pocketed the keys. "Funny. Ritchie Valens used to live 'round here," he said. "Before the asshole Mex died in that plane crash last month with the Big Bopper."

I smiled the smile that I'd perfected in case any talent scouts were ever around. "Funny. You know all the right people."

He came around to my side of the car and opened the door. He pointed my gun at me, saying, "Please," with a politeness that surprised me, then, "Don't give me a reason to use this."

We walked through the twilight together, past some rusted farm equipment, a couple of late-model cars, then up the wooden steps to the front door of the house.

The screen door squeaked and slammed shut as we

went in. I smelled Cuban cigar smoke and fried eggs.

The room was rustic western with furniture made from rough pieces of timber. Indian blankets hung from the walls at angles. Faint trails of smoke went up the chimney of a stone fireplace. An ancient Atwater-Kent radio stood in the corner quietly singing to itself. I think I heard Patsy Cline and "Just a Closer Walk with Thee."

Three men sat at a table, playing cards. I knew two of them. One was Frankie "Troca" Trocadero. The second was the goateed protester, who'd chanted about bombs and gas outside Edwards Air Force Base. The third was a fat man dressed like a farm hand in red checked shirt and blue bib overalls.

My driver shoved me farther into the room. Troca put down his cigar, came toward me, and spoke my name.

I straightened and spoke his back, trying to appear to be toughest guy in the room. "Where's Mickey?"

Troca looked at me like I was from the forty-ninth state. He had a habit of moving his head from side to side, limbering up a stiff neck. "Who'd you say?"

I shook my arms to get some blood flowing, but which made the handcuffed behind my back rattle like cheap jewelry. "You know who I mean. Mickey Cohen. Your boss. You wouldn't do anything without his blessing. Where is he?"

Troca smiled and laugh lines appeared beside his dark brown eyes, which was not the reaction I was going for. "Mickey couldn't make it, shithead." He wiped his thick lips with the fingertips of his right hand and looked back at the other two guys who had moved to stand near the fireplace. "Seems that he dropped a bar of soap on his toe in the shower and broke it."

I chuckled. "The soap? Or the shower?"

He was quick, which worried me. "No, shit-for-brains. The toe." He planted his right fist deep in my stomach, knocking me to the floor.

I resisted a powerful urge to throw up.

These clowns were so confident now that they unlocked my cuffs. That worried me, too.

Troca stood over me, helping me into a chair. I continued to control the urge and watched through watery eyes, as they stood over me like vultures.

I shuddered and took as deep a breath as I could.

Troca reached back over to the table for his cigar. "Now that we understand each other, we're going to have a little talk, Wade," he said. "You start."

Fat man chuckled with his mouth closed.

Up to now, I'd considered Troca to be small time nothing in gangdom. Mickey was known for assembling a crew of somewhat loyal lieutenants and underlings. He'd once had a group of mugs that the press and police called "the seven dwarfs." Troca was one of the new regime of hardcase bookies and young hoods who hoped for a piece of the easy action and to create some honor for themselves among thieves. Now that Mickey was away in

Washington—possibly never to return—Troca seemed to be trying to better his lot by making a bold land grab for a piece of Cohen's territory.

I watched while Driver pulled my .38 Special from his coat pocket. It made me nervous enough to start fiddling with the Twist-o-Flex band of my wristwatch.

Troca leaned over and blew smoke in my face. "Talk to me, before I pound the crap out of you, just on principle."

Nausea welled up in me again and I held on to an ideal I'd once read—to be the best man in my world and a good enough man for any world.

Then I puked on his shoes. Just on principle.

"Jesus fuckin' Christ!"

CHAPTER 9

ands shoved me deep into a chair. Driver set my gun on the mantle and got a rag from somewhere to help wipe off Troca's soiled footwear. I hoped that I'd also gotten through to his socks, but it didn't look like it. Troca pulled off one shoe and then the other, but his socks looked clean. As he stood there in his stocking feet, I knew I had him right where I wanted him. Yeah, sure.

He turned back to me and growled like a wild animal, reaching into his elegant jacket and bringing out a 9 mm automatic.

I was so close to getting it, I could smell the flowers. My head felt like it did when I woke up after sleeping all night in the LA smog. I cleared my eyes, ears, nose, and throat and struggled to keep from clearing my bowels. I rubbed my wrists, dry-washed my face, and tried to bargain. "You know, if Mickey were here, he'd offer to buy me off."

Troca waved his gigantic gun. "Too bad for you, Wade." The barrel looked like a howitzer. "Mickey's not here and I'm not Mickey. Now talk, dammit, before I start to count at you."

I took a deep breath to settle myself in the low-slung chair. "I'm investigating the death of a test pilot for the air force. Guy named Taffe." I gestured with my chin and tried a bluff. "Your friend there knows him."

Behind my back, a cuckoo clock went off, but it didn't stop the goatee guy from coming forward.

"I don't know what he's talking about," he claimed over top of the nine or ten silly sounds of the clock. "He's figured out that the protestors are linked to us and that'll screw up the whole thing."

"Shuddup," Troca barked.

I spat a sour gob onto the planed-wood floor and looked up, "What whole thing?"

Goatee stepped between us and I almost saw my chance. His brow was tight with nervous energy and his eyes held flecks of hazel. "He was at Reliance yesterday, snooping around, asking questions," he explained to Troca. "He knows, I tell you. He knows beaucoup."

Troca moved his head to loosen his neck and shoulders again. "Hell. I don't know what that means, but maybe you're right. Maybe he does know too much."

Fat Man moved closer, grinning his big lips like a fool. I thought he was going to try and drool me to death.

They studied me like I was a bug, and I looked again into the single dark eye of Troca's gun. "If you want an easy death, you're going to tell us everything," he said. "Right now."

My mind raced, looking for an exit, while the radio quietly played music-to-get-your-butt-kicked-by in the background and something moved in the hallway behind the three men. Whatever I said next, it needed to be convincing. They weren't going to make stupid mistakes.

Goatee was feeling bold. He drummed the fingertips of his right hand against his thigh, as if he had an itch beneath the skin. "Yeah, blow your cool, man, and tell us everything, before we sink you and your car into the bottom of the Bouquet Reservoir."

I gave that some serious thought. "So, is that what you did to Johnny Sunset?"

They were quiet. Bingo. Then Troca fired his gun at me. The bullet smacked the chair behind my head and nicked my left ear. I could feel blood running down the side of my face.

"That's it," I shouted. "That's it. You're off my Christmas list."

Troca smirked, moved his head from side to side, and pointed his nine-millimeter at my heart. I watched his trigger finger turn white and the hammer fall.

CLICK.

Nothing happened, except for Goatee's grin scissoring through his beard.

I think I felt my heart in my throat, or maybe it was more vomit.

They all leaned over me again, laughing in idiot delight.

"Don't go cowboy on us, Wade," Troca said. "Nobody knows you're here. It'll be real easy."

A slight figure crept behind them toward the mantle and my gun. It seemed to float there for hours, like a Boeing 707 making a runway approach. Finally, I launched up at a jack-in-the-box angle, slamming my forehead under Troca's chin. Something crunched in the left side of my face and my vision flared. Troca's gun went off and so did mine. Driver screamed in mortal pain.

"Go. Go," Suzi screamed.

I screamed, "You go!" and kicked the automatic from Troca's hand.

Suzi went out the squeaking screen door. I plowed into Goatee in my best blocking move, felt a stab from my trick shoulder. Fat man tried to block my path to the door, but I slammed into his gut and managed to yank away his gun, while following Suzi into the dark front yard.

We ran, heads down, for cover into the darkened barn. My nose caught the odors of wet hay and moist horseshit as we stumbled through the old building to dash out the back into the crisp night air. There were loud shouts and at least two shots in our direction. We rounded the side of the barn together, trying to gain the Kaiser.

I fired the Fat man's gun into the darkness in the direction of the farmhouse. A scream rang out. Into the open yard fell a writhing shape, clutching at itself. Other voices cursed and shouted.

We ran for my car. I tried to stretch my facial muscles to check for damage on the left side of my head, but nothing felt like it was moving.

"Rip his ass!" someone yelled from behind us.

Suzi grabbed my arm and pulled me to the car. "You're hurt. I'll drive. Give me the keys."

"The spare is under the right fender," I told her, feeling for the little magnetic box as she got in.

Two more shots rang out in my direction. I felt a burning pain on the back of my left hand that shocked my system so much that I dropped the gun. Then I didn't feel my left hand at all. Suzi had the car door open and the dome light drew fire like moths. I shoved her over to the passenger side of the Kaiser and slid in behind the wheel. A bullet spidered the driver's side rear window as I got the key in the ignition and gunned the engine. "Where's your car?"

"Back down the road. Leave it."

Another shot banged into the passenger side of the car. I tried to navigate the dark, dirt road with my good hand and eye. "Where the hell is your back up?"

"Out of town," she shouted. "Watch out for that tree."

I almost swung the car over on its side, racing around a curve. "They'll be after us in a second and they know the roads."

"No they won't," she said, firing back at them "I let the air out of their tires. What do you think took me so long?"

Yet another shot rang out from up on the hillside to our right. It sounded like a rifle.

Suzi's window shattered. Her face froze and blood began to flower from her neck and shoulder.

☙❧

We whizzed past her car on the side of the road and drove farther down the hill like Jimmy Reece at last year's Indy 500. I immediately remembered that his car had sailed fifty feet into the air, landed upside down, and burst into flames.

"Suzi," I called to her, slowing as I pulled left onto the two-lane highway.

She didn't respond.

I tapped the brakes again and reached over for her. The gun clattered from her hand to the floorboards. Her blue eyes fluttered and blood continued to seep from her right shoulder.

I grabbed the car phone from the dash and dialed

"0." After a few seconds of static in my right ear, I heard a small female voice: "Operator."

"Thank God. I've got a wounded woman here in my car and need directions to the Palmdale hospital. They have one, right?"

I banked the next turn and gunned the engine into a long straightaway.

"I'm sorry, sir," the voice said. "You say that you're calling from within your car, sir?"

I blew past a sign that read, *Palmdale – 8 Miles* and saw a red weal that had been seared across my hand.

"Hurry, operator. I'm eight miles out, heading west, I think."

The glare of approaching headlights almost blinded my right eye.

Crackle. "Palmdale General is located on Desert Valley Drive."

I didn't think we could make it, but I had to try. I slammed the accelerator to the floorboards, goosing every mph from the flathead-six engine. "Can you give me directions?"

More static. "I'm sorry, sir. I do not have that information."

It felt like a fish bone was constricting my throat. I let the phone drop from my shoulder. A mental flash of my parents' death raced before me. I absolutely *hated* driving at night on back roads. "Suzi!"

Ahead on the left was another sign. Palmdale Engine

House No. 3. I eased back on the gas pedal and skidded into the wide driveway of the fire station.

I wasn't sure I was breathing.

CHAPTER 10

Beep. Beep.

Random thoughts circled my mind like orbiting satellites.

Beep. Beep.

They had Suzi hooked up to a device to monitor her vital signs.

The Palmdale hospital was testing a telemetry machine for a nearby company called Spacelabs. I'd been told that the machine was under development so that the biological team at Edwards could keep track of an astronaut's heart rate. I guess the old guy with the mobile teeth at the Skelly gas station had been right and just about all the folks in the area worked with or for the US Air Force.

Beep. Beep.

The bandage to protect my left eye was wrapped clear around my head, almost like a turban. I was glad I'd given up wearing a hat last year.

An ophthalmologist had told me that there had been no penetrating fracture to my orbital ridge and only minor damage to my left retina. He'd sutured the tear in my skin above my eye and bandaged me up, giving me some pain pills and an eye patch to wear while things healed.

My head, shoulder, left hand, and stomach ached, but I'd live. The hand was patched with soft, white gauze.

Beep. Beep.

But maybe Suzi wouldn't.

They'd gotten the rifle round out of her, but she'd lost a lot of blood, been in shock, and was currently "non-responsive." They had her in a semi-darkened room in the Intensive Care Unit, laying on a clean, white bed, with a breathing tube in her throat and the monitor wired to her pale body. There was a bag of blood and glass bottle of clear liquid dripping into her. I sat there listening to her breathing and the beeping machine, while every few minutes a doctor or night nurse came in to check on things.

Beep. Beep.

I dry-swallowed one of the pain pills, but was certain that my pain was nothing compared to hers. But the pain that really got to me—the agony that pounded in my head and heart was the pain that I'd caused her. I couldn't get away from the thought that I should have been able to help her without her getting hurt. My plan was that I'd be a hero again for her, but in the end, she had saved me and now might die for it.

It wasn't that I wanted to be a hero again for her. It was that I wanted to do something that mattered, instead of being tarnished with fear and failure.

I went outside to clear my head and smoke a cigarette. Beep, beep. "Luckies are cleaner, fresher, smoother." Beep, beep. "Kools are a breath of fresh air." Beep, beep. "Salem, springtime fresh." The damn thing burned my throat and tasted like shit.

I went and sat in my darkened car in the hospital parking lot.

Mr. P's .38 was on the floor. I reached down with my good hand, past the bits of shattered window glass. The firearm rested in my open palm and, for the first time in my life, I saw the six simple steps it would take to use this thing to fire a chunk of lead into my brain.

One, put my finger on the trigger.

Two, turn my wrist toward my body.

Three, tighten my grip against the recoil.

Four, raise the gun to my head.

Five, press the muzzle against my temple.

Six, jerk the trigger and…

It was so real that it frightened me. It frightened me so much that I didn't think I could actually do it.

I tried step one and felt the coolness of the trigger on my fingertip.

I watched in fascination as I took step two and twisted a wrist that didn't seem to be mine.

Steps three and four came together at once in a single, smooth motion.

My hand began to tremble so much that I had trouble finding my temple.

I felt the throb of my heart beat down the length of the barrel, but my fist continued to hold the gun in place.

The deadly weapon began to grow heavy. My arm began to sag. My palm opened again and I stared at Mr. P's revolver lying there as light as a handful of shaving cream.

I could feel my heart rate returning to normal. I could never use his gun in this way. I looked at it in wonder, as if he had reached out and pushed it from me.

The early morning air felt cool in the car with the shot-out passenger-side window. This would never do for a serious, methodical detective.

I shook myself, as if from a dream, and even smiled a little, thinking perversely that I'd just pushed myself into a moment of high drama worthy of Hitchcock. But that didn't change my conviction that I had better things to do with this gun. Things like using it to unlock doors and help get the answers.

That was what the gun was for. And, in a way, that was what I was for, too. If I did it right; if I did it with honor, I'd justify my actions, myself, and my chosen path.

I fumbled out another smoke and lit it with the car lighter. "Be happy. Go Lucky."

CHAPTER 11

What happened to your head?"

The breathing tube was out of her mouth now and the bed was cranked up a little so she could gaze around the room and settle on me.

I scooched my chair closer and she touched my left cheek, causing me to wince somewhat from the pain. "Cut myself shaving," I smiled.

She snorted and winced in return.

"Do you remember what happened?" I asked, trying and gauge her response.

She signed. "Of course, I remember." Her left hand came up to her throat and she gave a faint cough. "I'm just not in the mood for your sense of humor."

I offered her a plastic glass of water. She sipped

slowly from the straw, almost matching the quieted pulse of the monitor. Norman would have loved to take it apart to find out what made it beep.

She finished swallowing the liquid and took a shallow breath. "It's nothing to joke about."

"I know. Sorry."

Her deep blues gazed into mine and then she seemed to drift away again. Her eyes opened wider. "You know what?" she said, as if she'd lost track of the conversation.

"What?"

"No. I mean what—what is it that you know?"

"I know that it's no joke," I admitted, not sure we were making any progress here.

She nodded slightly. "Right. No joke. Deadly serious, Standy. They killed Johnny and I know it now."

I set the water glass back down on the table beside her bed. "Is that why you followed me? To get proof?"

She lowered her eyes and nodded ever so slightly.

I sighed. "Thanks for being there for me, but don't ever do it again."

She tightened her face and didn't look up.

"Just get well," I advised her. "And I'll see about getting the police to search the reservoir for—" I stopped my big mouth and changed the subject. "It's about twenty miles west of here, near Angeles National Forest."

Nevertheless, a small tear formed and gently trickled down her pale cheek. I caught it with my thumb and felt the tide coming in to my left eye a bit, too. "You never should have gotten into this detective business, Suzi." It was almost exactly what Lex had told me earlier.

She sniffled. "Neither should you. It's crazy. Dangerous. You guys don't need to prove yourselves and take all these chances."

We both grew quiet, considering our various bandaged states. The smell of antiseptic and alcohol drifted into our souls. The beep went on.

"I was following your lead," she said, clearing her throat.

"What? What lead?"

"Your lead into this detective business." She came at it from another direction. "Back when we were kids that one summer at the dude ranch, you got all excited about being a private eye."

I knew the exact moment that she meant, but I was stunned to learn now the effect it might have had on her. I'd gotten lost in the neighboring hills and had sprained my ankle when the search party found me. It'd all caused me to be laid up in my bunk for almost a week, while the rest of the camp had gone on with their horseback riding and calf roping.

There had been nothing for me to do, except lie there, listen to the radio, and kill time reading old books and magazines.

"It was something I read at the time," I told her. "I know it sounds dumb now to tell you this, but—" I glanced up.

Two CHP men came into the room with guns holstered.

☙❧

When I'd first arrived with Suzi last night, I'd been quizzed by the doctors and the hospital security staff. I'd explained frantically what had happened and they had immediately reported the incident to the California Highway Patrol. Now, I was shaking hands with Patrolmen Hensel and Williams. They wore starched uniform shirts with six-pointed badges, plastic nametags, and short, black ties held in place by straight, brass clips. Both men had tucked their caps under left armpits, but I could still see the flying-wheel insignia on the crowns of their headgear.

Hensel carried a clipboard and was already making notes. Williams seemed to be the lead man and he turned our handshake into a minor endurance trial. He finally let go and stepped past me to look down at Suzi, who had relaxed back into slumber.

Turning his head to face me, Williams silently mouthed, "How is she?"

I jerked my head, indicating that we should leave the room, almost bumping into Hensel, as I looked back to be sure that Suzi was breathing comfortably.

Out in the hallway, I told them that the doctors said it was still touch-and-go.

"You're a private investigator?" Williams asked. He was chewing spearmint gum and I got a whiff of it, while I showed him my state license and the permit for my gun. "So, tell me, Mr. Wade," he said, "exactly what happened?"

"To my head?"

He didn't miss a beat. "To your head. To your lady friend. The whole thing."

I explained in some detail and watched their expressions out of the corner of my one eye.

Hensel sort of laughed. "You got knocked out? I thought private eyes got cracked on the head every day like there was nothing to it." He was chewing, too.

Williams took over. "So, that's how she was shot? Rescuing you?"

"What's your point, Officer?"

His expression grew cold. "You carry a .38?"

I reached under my arm and brought it out, handing it to him.

He sniffed the barrel. "It's been fired."

"Like I already explained, she got it away from them and fired in self-defense. You should see the bullet holes in my car."

"Okay, Mr. Wade. We'll keep this for now."

"Sure. Uh, do I get a receipt?"

"Sure. Harry is writing one up for you now. Let's go look at your car."

We went out into the parking lot, past their black-

and-white Buick Century, to where my battered Kaiser sat. The patrolmen walked around it and looked inside like they were considering buying it. Hensel even kicked a tire when he wrote down the plate number. Then they came back to stand with me under the shade of a large hibiscus bush.

Williams hitched up his web belt and holster. "And you say you were abducted by three men?"

I gave them Troca's name and described the other two men. Hensel scribbled.

"We'll check with LAPD," he said. "You need to know that we've sent a couple of patrolmen up to the ranch in Lost Valley. They radioed in that no one was there, but they found traces of blood and few fresh bullet holes, along with spent shells from a Winchester .405 rifle. The hospital says that's the caliber of the round taken from Mrs. Sunset's shoulder."

"Did they find her car?"

"Yes, her gray Plymouth sedan was parked down the road from the ranch. If you don't mind my asking, what exactly is your relationship to her?"

I was ready for that question, but I decided to give them a straight answer. "Nothing special, Officer. She's an old friend. She asked me to meet with these guys and it got out of hand."

Hensel didn't buy it. "I'll say it did."

I thought about Walt, the dead astronaut, Reliance Management Corporation, Johnny Sunset, and how complex it had all become. I needed to make it seem simple. "We were investigating her husband's disappearance. We think those three guys may have killed him. They thought we should be stopped."

Williams spit out his gum. "So, you had an old-fashioned shoot out. You and Mrs. Sunset were both injured and—if you were abducted, as you say—those three men are still out there. They'll be looking for you."

"Can you put a guard on her room?" He nodded. I realized that Williams was right. They could come after me any time now. They knew who I was and could quickly figure out where they might find me. "I get your point. Thanks. You'll want a formal report, right?" He nodded again. "But I'm not under arrest, right?" I asked.

He thought about it. "No, I guess not. You can go, if you want to."

"Thanks again. And I might need my gun back, for protection."

He thought about it some more. "Absolutely not."

"Remember, I have a permit."

"Forget it."

"And you know where to find me."

The wheels in his head started to turn.

"Come on, Officer. *They* know how to find me, too."

Williams looked at Hensel. Hensel chewed and shrugged. Williams gave me back my .38. "Be careful out there."

I signed an accident report and a carbon copy of the

statement Hensel had been writing. When I handed it back, it was all I could do to resist saying, "Ten-four."

popo

It was clear that I needed to get back to my boat immediately. There was every chance that Troca and company were already in pursuit of me. The *Cervantes II* would be their first stop.

As I sped back through Antelope Valley and put the San Gabrial Mountains over my left shoulder, I dearly hoped to see a road sign that read, "Leaving Trouble Behind," but it didn't happen.

I tried to remember if Lex planned to be at the boat. I tried to use the car phone to call Norman, so he could contact Lex, but the mountains seemed to block the reception. I tried to use my good eye to see around a convoy of oil tanker trucks that hung in front of me on the highway for twenty minutes. My hatred of traffic was high under normal driving conditions. Now, I swore and honked and ground my teeth, but it did little good.

Finally, I drove down Route 99 into the North Valley as the noon news came on the radio. Lou Costello had died from a heart attack. Fabian would appear on the Perry Como show. ABC-TV had canceled "The Mickey Mouse Club," which, on top of everything else, reminded me that I needed to check in with Walt.

It was 1:30 on an overcast afternoon, before I braked

at the dock and saw Lex's pickup truck. I ran up the gangplank.

"Hiya, squirrel. What happened to your head?"

"Never mind my head. How long you been here?"

She blinked dumbly at me and heaved a coil of tubing from her shoulder to the deck. "About ten minutes. You needed new hoses on the starboard bilge pump, why?"

So the boat had been empty all morning. There was a faint smell in the sea air that made my nostrils twitch—a familiar, acrid smell. Gasoline. "Don't turn anything on or light a match."

We carefully moved to the aft deck engine area. The odor was stronger back there. Too strong. The engine cover was half off. Beside it sat an open Sunkist orange crate and it was ticking. Fastened inside the crate was a wind-up alarm clock laying face down. Its winding key was wired to the trigger of a Roy Rogers cap gun, also bolted to the bottom of the crate. The toy was breached open to allow for a maximum of sparks when the alarm went off and the gun fired. It was an assemblage of innocent parts, which explosive investigators would never suspect. And we had no idea when the alarm clock was set to go off.

Lex was on my left side so I couldn't see her clearly. "Shit fire," she breathed and grabbed the crate, manhandling it to the upper deck while pushing me aside. She was so intent on getting the device overboard that she slipped and tumbled into the muddy water on the port side away from the dock, still holding the crate with both hands.

I called out a brilliant observation. "Hey!"

The ocean smoothed above Lex and I started kicking off my shoes.

Her head broke the surface and she spat a stream of water. She coughed and swam steady strokes around the cruiser to the pier, pulling herself up next to a pylon.

I followed. "Are you okay?"

She wiped water off her face with a broad hand. "So are you going to answer my question?"

I gave her my confused face. "What question?"

"Your head. What happened to your head?"

I laughed so hard that I had to hold my stomach like Harpo.

She came back up the gangplank. "Come on, squirrel. We gotta find that gas leak and fan the place out to get rid of the fumes."

I stopped laughing and got to work.

❧

While we cleared the air, I gave her a brief summary.

"You're doing it again," she growled. "We don't have time for long explanations. Those damn rats could be watching us right now from anywhere on shore."

I peered out a porthole, but saw nothing suspicious.

"As soon as we're done here, you take the boat out and moor it somewhere so they can't find it, like Malibu Beach. We don't want to go through this ever again."

"Belay that," Lex said, shaking her head. "The word is that they're still filming that surfing movie, "Gidget," up there."

"What's a gidget?"

Lex shrugged. "Girl midget? Anyway, I know of a dock down at Redondo Beach that's open. I'll take her there. You head over to the Georgian and see Marvin about a room."

I knew where the Georgian Hotel was in Santa Monica. Marvin Cramer, Lex's old bar mate and night manager there, owed a favor from an earlier case and could probably get me a room without registering.

When we finished fanning the air with boat cushions, I wrote a number on a slip of paper and handed it to her. "Call me when you get the boat to a safe harbor."

She looked at the paper. "This is what?"

"Norman installed a car phone in my car. It works pretty good—sometimes."

"Geez," she said, wadding the paper into the damp pocket of her coveralls. "Just be careful, all right?" She shook her graying head. "I don't want to have to tell the chief that you're dog meat."

Me too neither.

ᔕᓇᔕ

As Lex backed the *Cervantes II* out of the lagoon, I drove my Kaiser Manhattan through Venice to the San Diego Freeway, exiting onto Olympic and cruising into Santa Monica. I took my time, turning right onto Twenti-eth Street and toured around the square blocks between Euclid Avenue and Lincoln Park. The cloud layer made the smog heavy and my head ached. The bandage on my head seemed secure. I probably was, too.

Norman's voice on the car phone sounded like one of those Alvin chipmunks, but the damn thing actually worked.

"Where are you?" he squeaked.

"Never mind."

"When are you coming back?"

"I'll let you know. The phone seems to work okay, but not always."

"Roger, Mr. Wade. And *Mechanix Illustrated* is go-ing to publish a story about my check-cashing camera."

I had no idea what he was talking about.

"And I've got some new chapters for you to read."

"Can't wait." I hung up and watched the people driv-ing or walking home from work and catching or getting off buses. No one seemed to be following me, so I headed over to Ocean Avenue and the hotel.

The Georgian was an eight-story art deco structure that faced the fresh sea air and claimed to have hosted Chaplin, Gable, and Lombard, just not all at the same time. Marvin got me a third-floor ocean-side room that was scheduled to get new carpet and a fresh coat of paint next week. He bragged that it was right below where Bugsy Siegel used to stay and rumor had it that Al Capone kept a moll in that very room back in the late '20s. I didn't buy a word of it, but was eternally grateful for a place to grab a shower.

It was impossible to wash around the bandages. The one on my hand sloughed off to expose a raw scrape that would leave a diagonal scar from pinky to thumb. My head bandage got soggy on one side and the adhesive tape began to come loose. Gingerly, I unwound the wad of gauze and tape and studied my left eye in the mirror. The view was blurry and the side of my face was the color of a ripe prune, like I'd been sucker punched by Rocky Marciano.

There was swelling and loops of black thread stitched between the lid and the brow. I crinkled my face in a grin to see how much it would hurt. A lot. I probed the stitches with my fingertips and that hurt more.

I swallowed a couple of scarlet-and-gray Darvon capsules for the pain and dug out the eye patch. It was black and had an elastic band to wrap around your head. The patch settled easily over my left eye and the strap paralleled the white streak in my hair.

Studying myself in the mirror, I decided I could direct a movie, since I now looked like Fritz Lang, John Ford, and Raoul Walsh.

I decided that Orson Welles should start wearing one

of these things. Maybe he had while making *Citizen Kane* or the opening of *Touch of Evil.*

I looked over at the curtained hotel room window, trying to judge distances. It seemed that I could get around okay, since I was able to dress without barging into the furniture. Gradually, I let more light into the room by opening the window curtains. I watched the people below walk along the beach across the street. The cloud-covered waves pawed the beach in easy breakers and a few seagulls drifted like kites. It would take some getting used to, but I'd be able to navigate with the patch.

I sat down on the edge of the bed and reached for the room phone without knocking over the lamp. When I dialed Walt's private number, there was no answer. For all I knew, he could have been on the moon.

I thought about taking a nap in the quiet of the late afternoon, but remembered that the Santa Monica Library was only a couple of blocks over from the hotel, and I sure needed mucho information, if I had any hopes of success with this case. Heaving my bones up and adjusting my patch, I ambled out through the parking lot, in search of the dubious information resources of "Bay City."

CHAPTER 12

Pardon me, miss. Do you have any books by, um, Willy Ley?"

She did not look up, but instead pulled a pencil from her hair and pointed. "You could check the card catalog, sir, but I think you'll find them in the 629s. They're in the room to your—" She locked onto my eye patch and her face reddened. "—your left."

"Thank you."

For the next hour and a half, I scanned through various books, newspapers, and magazines concerning some pretty neat stuff. I got out my pad and started making notes.

It was no secret that the Russians had jumped ahead in the "Space Race," ever since the successful launch of their first Sputnik into orbit around the Earth back in late 1957. It was a "pearl-harbor" moment. America's biggest problem was that our rocket efforts had been spread across three military branches: army, navy, and air force. But now with the establishment of the National Aeronautics and Space Administration, things were beginning to be consolidated and coordinated into a single program, and information was starting to be shared among the branches. The fact that NASA was a civilian organization also signaled to the world that the missile and space activities of the US were for non-military purposes.

Now, under the motto: "Ever Upward," the nation's Project Mercury was an intensive program to go higher and faster, mobilizing creative science and technology to orbit and retrieve a manned satellite.

It had begun at many times and places, but the focus was currently on the new X-15 rocket plane that would take off and land from Rogers Dry Lake at Edwards. This fifty-foot long missile-shaped vehicle with an unusual wedge-shaped vertical tail and thin stubby wings, manned by a test pilot like Captain Taffe, would drop from a B-52 bomber and soar up over sixty miles into the thin atmosphere at speeds approaching 4,000 mph on engines fueled with liquid ammonia and oxygen. Then it would glide down to Earth and land at 200 mph on the dry lakebed, to be used over and over again like a shuttle to space.

These same tough-gut test pilots would be America's first astronauts. With their anticipated success, these men would symbolize the country's hopes and fears for reaching out and achieving another rung upward on the vertical ladder. They would cast off gravity's physical and mental moorings and sail into one of mankind's greatest adventures, the exploration of near space.

I located almost no information on the test pilots themselves and, of course, nothing specific to Captain Albert Taffe. Perhaps Scott or Kirkman could let me view his personnel file at the air base.

ⒸⓈⒸⓈ

My stomach began to growl so loud that I thought the librarian would throw me out.

On the way back to the Georgian, I found a local hardware store next to a Vons market and bought a small wisk broom, a roll of packaging tape, and a sheet of milky plastic. Working with it all in the hotel parking lot, I soon had the front seat of my car swept and the passenger window patched nearly as well as my eye. At least the wing window still opened and closed.

By the time I got done sweating through all that, I was hungry enough to eat my spare tire, so I went down to the Red Griffin Room in the Georgian's basement and stuffed myself on salad, lamb chops, and au gratin potatoes. That and a half-bottle of Bordeaux set me back almost five bucks with tip, but it was worth it to taste the excellent cooking of master chef Victor Bruzzi. Staying at the Georgian was a good plan. The stately hotel was high-class enough that I was certain the Organization would not think to look for a low-class guy like me here.

Between the wine and the pain pills, my head started swimming. I dog paddled up to my room and switched on the black-and-white television. Surprise, surprise. Guy Williams was doing his Zorro bit again. He carved a "Z" on Garcia's cummerbund, saluted with the hilt of his sword, and dashed off across the prison roof tiles. It all looked like grand fun to me. Then there was some historical fiction about Wyatt Earp, an ad for four-hour cold tablets, and Pat Boone hosting his twin, Tab Hunter. My mind wandered through government contracts for Reliance Management and how a dead test pilot could be connected to protestors at Edwards.

I needed to find my way through this inky mess. It was like being surrounded by a thick, dark haze. Off in the distance, I heard a horse whiny. Out of the fog, Suzi rode up, her arm in a sling. She pulled a cap gun and shot a tarantula off a birthday cake. I waved an old magazine at her, trying to capture her attention, but her horse turned into Security Officer Scott, and the two of them walked off, hand in hand. It didn't seem fair or patriotic and I wanted to go after them, but I couldn't get up because of my sprained ankle. A baggy-dressed, black-and-white clown with clocks on his socks came to attention before me, saluted, and yanked me up.

The end of the Star-Spangled Banner roused me to

half wakefulness. I stumbled to the bathroom and then came back and shut off the fuzzy TV static. Within seconds, I was back in bed, oozing slowly into sleep.

❧❧❧

And yet, as much as life seems so peculiar and loony-toon, some things remain fixed points in the center of a changing universe.

The dream I'd had the night before spurred me on to fulfill a promised task the next morning. As had been my custom over the last few months, I put the column stick shift into drive and rolled over to the Hollywood Medical Center to visit Gunther Wherthman. For over half a century, he had lived his life as a little man no more than three feet tall, but in recent years, his dwarfism had slowly begun to take its toll, leaving him arthritic, hunched, and in constant pain.

"Stanley, it is good to see you again," he said beneath his breathing mask.

His lungs had begun to fail in the last few months and we both knew that they would soon take him down all the way into the big sleep.

"Good to see you, too, Gunther. Here, I brought you something." I placed a blue paperbound Swiss edition of Heinrich Zimmer's *Philosophies of India* into his frail, but steady hands. It was the last book he'd worked on several years back.

"Ah, the Bollingen Series from Princeton. Joseph Campbell edited Zimmer's lectures and I brought them back into the German. Wherever did you find a copy of this rare edition?"

I felt my face grow warm. "I'm a detective. It's what I do. Although, lately, I'm not doing it very well."

He nodded as much as possible beneath his fogging mask. "I understand. You always wanted to be the hero in your own life story, Stanley. The Buddha would tell you that true heroics come from joyful participation in the sorrows of the workplace. You must be patient and for-giving."

We both said nothing for a few minutes, giving him time to catch his breath. Gunther had assisted Mr. P for years before I came along, providing insight, knowledge, and encouragement, as he was doing for me now.

"This is a sad time for India, Nepal, and the Buddhist religion. I read that the Dalai Lama is under attack from the Chinese. But, believe me, whatever happens, it will be for the best. That does not mean that we should not try to make life better. Just accept the changes that come and work with them every day."

The character of the man was astounding. He was the only person I'd met in the last two days who had resisted the urge to ask about my head or eye patch. "I know, Gunther." My heart thumped in my chest and my good eye started to blur a little. "You guys were there for me when I needed you and I'm here for you now."

His German accent seemed stronger than ever when he repeated, "Joyful participation."

I thought about it for a moment. It was like a common man's nobility, to live in an imperfect world and yet try to make something right, if not perfect. The little man in front of me had spent his life translating what seemed like gibberish into clarity and meaning. I guessed that I could try and do the same in my profession.

I held his small hand and told him that I looked forward to visiting him again soon.

He held up an open palm. "We shall see. In the meantime, as the other Indians would say, 'walk with grace.'" And damned if he didn't wink at me.

☙❧

An intensely bright beam of light flared into my eye, causing me to see pink and yellow blood vessels.

"It's called an onthalmoscope," the doctor said, stepping back to display the silver flashlight device with its pointy funnel.

"I know a guy who'd love to get his hands on one," I said. "Probably convert it into a ray gun."

I had stopped earlier in the morning for a breakfast bagel at Zucky's Deli and then had taken the long drive again back up the Valley. The aggravating traffic had been heavy for a Friday morning, so I calmed myself by listening to golden oldies of the big band era on the radio.

Glenn Miller, Artie Shaw, and the Dorsey brothers. Johnny Mathis sang "Fly Me to the Moon." He was warbling, "Let me know what spring is like on Jupiter and Mars" when I parked at the hospital to visit Suzi and check on my eye.

"Okay, it looks like you won't lose it," the doctor said, "but there's been severe damage to the area and you'll need to continue wearing the patch for the next month."

"Aye-aye, captain," I said. "Now, can yea look at me aching shoulder?"

He stepped back. "What's wrong with your shoulder?"

"Old college football injury."

He sniffed. "Orthopedics is down the hall to your right."

"Just kidding, Doc. Thanks."

He sniffed again. Maybe I had BO.

❧❦❧

They had moved her to a private room in the east wing of the hospital. I hesitated at the door, because a pair of beige slacks and tasseled, brown leather loafers stood beneath the light blue privacy curtain that surrounded her bed. I came forward and heard a man clear his throat.

He was wearing one of those Bing Crosby hats with

the little feather in the band, but it was pushed back on his head and I could see that he was balding. He had a florid face and a large, flat nose. His ears didn't look much bigger than a child's.

"And you are?" I asked.

He turned and I noticed that he had cop's eyes and blond hair sprouting from the open collar of his white, short sleeve shirt.

"Swan," he said, but didn't offer his hand. "George Swan. LAPD." His teeth were white and bright, like he used toothpaste with hexa-hexa-hexachlorophene. "And you are Stan Wade, right?"

I looked down at Suzi, resting. "How is she?"

He looked down at her, too, and took no interest in my eye patch. I assumed that the two of them had talked about me already. "You want to get a cup of coffee?"

We walked down the hall together and pulled scolding paper cups from a machine in a waiting room. The dark swill in mine burned the tip of my tongue, but he seemed fine with his.

"Her condition is improving," he began, "and we might be able to get her home in a day or so…" I must have been frowning, because he said, "What?"

"Where the hell were you when she was shot?"

"I thought she told you." He blinked. "I was back in Philly, attending a family funeral."

"Why did you drag her into this to begin with and then leave her alone and vulnerable?"

"She was already on the inside at Reliance, when she contacted us. She told us that she was trying to find out what happened to her husband. I couldn't have stopped her, if I'd wanted. Believe me, I tried."

It sounded possible, but I still didn't like it.

He took a slug of swill. "She knew Worthmyer somehow from their past. It gave us a quick and easy in, so the Department assigned me to back her up. But we weren't supposed to take any action, except to observe and collect info. Now, let me ask you one: what were you doing there and how do you know her?"

I sipped my steaming brew, not because I was thirsty. "We go way back."

"Then you know she only has one speed. Forward."

I wondered just how well Swan, George Swan, knew Suzi, in order to be able to say that. "I'm working a confidential assignment for a client, but you need to know that she came to me for help—in your absence."

The muscles in his jaw tightened. "Yeah, well, I can protect her better than you can. So stand down now, Mr. Private Dick, or I'll have your license revoked in a heartbeat."

"You wanna take a step back, pal? You're standing on my foot."

I considered shoving him into a chair, but a nurse interrupted us. "She's calling for you."

Swan beat me back to the room and her side, asking, "Are you all right?"

I watched Suzi smile up at him. "Is everything all right back home?"

"Sure, sure," George said. "Don't concern yourself. I'm here now and the doctor's told me you could go home in a day or two. Good news, huh?"

I started to move forward from the doorway, when she said, "I need to talk to you in private."

He took her hand in his paws and looked at my single eye. She seemed to warm to his attention, like a cat being stroked. I scratched my left ear, winced, and chose discretion.

CHAPTER 13

Desert winds sweep across the Mojave, blowing powdery grit and tumbleweeds. I saw at least three trailers that had been overturned under a clear, unclouded sky.

The city of Lancaster hugged the open desert with these sun-baked mobile homes. Scrub-covered low hills nudged up against semiarid patches of alfalfa, almonds, and airplane plants. Rockwell, Lockheed, and Northrop. My parents had worked at Lockheed.

Now, there was a literal "aerospace boom" rolling across the city, but back in the 1930s, Indians had fought the Cavalry here in dozens of B movies. In 1942, B-24 cruisers had practiced bombing runs on a mock Japanese destroyer, the Muroc Maru, and the first jet plane was tested here soon after. By the late '40s, we'd broken the sound barrier and crashed the "flying wing" in this vast lakebed of parched silt.

There was a whole lot of history in this dancing, shimmering nothing. As I neared Edwards AFB, I thought I saw, far in the distance, a twenty-mule team hauling borax across the flats, but it turned out to be only a couple of twisty dust devils fooling my good eye.

At the base entry gate, I again heard the enraged roar of the jet engines. It appeared that the protestors were gone, which pleased me, since I wanted to avoid the beatnik goatee guy until I knew more and was in a better position to take him on.

I had called ahead for clearance and learned that Colonel Scott would be in a security meeting most of the afternoon.

"My God, man," Kirkman said, once we'd settled in his office. "With that eye patch, you remind me of the famous aviator, Wiley Post." His office was bigger than mine at the Brown Derby, but not by much. There were stacks of brochures and film canisters piled on the floor and the top of a row of filing cabinets. Rolled up promotional banners leaned against the open door to the darkened room next door.

I smiled. "I was hoping more to look like the Hathaway Shirt man," I said, explaining about my "self-inflected" head injury and trying not to sound too stupid. He took it all in, while filling and lighting a straight, cherry-wood pipe. I clicked my Zippo, set fire to a Lucky, and added to the cloud of smoke.

The room was without air conditioning, so I kept my tie loose. We exchanged notes about Project Mercury. I learned that the air force was hammering, gouging, and hauling away tons of rock and sand to lengthen the runway to more than twenty miles.

"We've got to get it long enough to accommodate the X-15," Kirkman said, gesturing with the stem of his pipe to a photo on the wall. "It's a huge job and we need all the help in the construction that we can get."

"Then I'd strongly suggest that you forget about getting it from the Reliance Management Corporation. Their kind of help will be a burden in the long run."

His brow tightened and then relaxed. "I guess that I'm not surprised. In fact, I told Scott last week that they were probably attached in some way to organized crime." He shrugged. "But he always wants to go full speed ahead and get things done, regardless of the means."

"I see. Well, let's just say that Reliance seems too closely associated with both the Mob and your protestors to do you any good. I haven't any solid proof to show you, but you'd be wise to conduct business with somebody else."

"Thank you for your insight, Mr. Wade," the major puffed. "I'll keep that in mind as we move forward."

I leaned over and stabbed out my cigarette in an ashtray on his cluttered desk. "So, how did the autopsy go?"

He grunted around his pipe stem and shuffled a few papers. Finally, he gave up searching. "Actually, there was no trace of any foreign substance in Captain Taffe's body. The medical examiner's report calls it death by drowning, just as we expected."

"Is the body still here?"

"No. His family arrived yesterday and had it transported back to their home in Iowa. Colonel Scott approved, since they seemed like good people. Taffe will be buried quietly with honors. We're not anxious to have the event covered by the press."

"What about the film in the security camera?"

"Good question."

A knock sounded on the office door behind me. Kirkman put down his pipe and raised an index finger to me as a signal to wait.

"Come in." The door opened and his face brightened. "Ah, Gordo. Come in, kid."

I turned and looked up at a medium-height man a little older than me, with wavy brown hair, blue eyes, and a crooked smile.

Kirkman got up and introduced us. "Mr. Wade, this is one of our candidates, Leroy Gordon Cooper. He'll probably take the X-15 up one of these days real soon."

"I wish," Cooper said in an Oklahoma drawl. "Nice to meet ya." We shook hands and looked straight into each other's eyes. Men among men.

Kirkman consulted a paper from a pile on his desk

and read, "His hobbies are photography, woodworking, boating, and fishing."

"And flying," Cooper added. "Call me Gordo."

"Mr. Wade, here, is a security consultant. As such, he may have some questions for you."

"Any time," Cooper grinned. "And you be sure and let me know if you want to go up in one of our F-104s."

I swallowed hard. Both men probably heard it. "Thanks. I'll pass for now."

The two airmen exchanged knowing looks. Then Cooper cleared his throat. "I was wondering, Rog, if you could get me some more of those official day passes. Trudy and the girls want to come see the *Star Lady* this weekend. Oh and could I also get about half a dozen of my test-pilot photos to autograph? The kids like to hand them out at school."

"Sure thing," Kirkman agreed. "Come on into the media room and I'll dig them out."

We all went through the adjoining door into a large windowless room where cardboard boxes were stacked on rows of folding chairs. Kirkman started rummaging into one of the brown cartons. "I give press briefings in here when the place isn't so cluttered."

I looked around the darkened room and spied a movie projector screen pulled halfway down to cover equations chalked on the blackboard behind it. Fanned out across the floor in a staggered spread was a loose stack of folders for the *Steve Canyon* TV show.

"You here because of what happened to Taffe?" Gordo asked me.

"Partly. What sort of man was he?"

"A-okay. Nice guy who's been on duty here at the base for over a year. Good pilot and downright a-okay."

"Here you go, kid." Kirkman handed Cooper the glossy eight-by-ten photos. "And I'll have the passes ready for you at the main desk by the end of the day."

"Thanks, Major." The test pilot turned back to me. "Nice meeting ya. Seems to me that we need all the security we can get around here."

"Good meeting you, too," I answered. "I'll do my best for the cause."

He gave me a two-finger salute and left.

Kirkman and I returned to his office and resumed our chat, just as another sonic boom pounded the building. I got out my pad and ballpoint pen from the Pep Boys. "You were going to tell me about the security film."

"Correct." Kirkman picked up his pipe and then put it back down. "According to Colonel Scott, the film that went to the outside lab was blank. We now think that Captain Taffe must have turned off the camera before committing suicide."

That was a jump. I immediately wondered why Taffe would take his own life. And why jimmy the camera beforehand? "I'd like to read his personnel file, if you don't mind."

"Yes, we anticipated that." Kirkman opened a draw

of his desk and carefully placed a folder before me. The cover said "Eyes Only," and there was a red paper band wrapped around it. "We've had to clear out a few passages about our operations here, but the un-classified information on the deceased is still here. You can keep the file for reference. It'll give you a good idea of what kind of man Taffe was."

I clicked my pen and was putting it and my notepad back into my jacket pocket just as Colonel Fielding Scott came into the office un-announced. Rank had its privileges.

"Have we got this thing wrapped up yet, Roger?" the security officer asked.

I was beginning to feel like I was in a tag-team match with no one on my side to tag. I rose up from my chair to address Scott. "Why are we switching to suicide, Colonel? Based on what evidence?"

My direct approach, and probably my eye patch, stopped him for a second. He touched his mustache and stood his ground. "Based on the damn lack of any other evidence, mister. Plus the fact, that I now know that Captain Taffe was troubled by events in his personal life."

"Remember, Mr. Wade," Kirkman added, "For the sake of the project, we need to avoid any negative publicity."

"That's batshit," I told them.

"I've spoken to the commander in chief and he concurs," Scott said.

My eyes widened, causing the left one sting. "The president?"

"He wants us to keep this under wraps, until such time as we've finished evaluating all the facts."

"Eisenhower?"

"Correct. Eisenhower is the president," Kirkman said,

I said, "Ike, eh?" and sat down.

Scott started giving orders. "I've also checked with the man who hired you and we all want you to take the report in this folder and investigate Taffe's residence and lifestyle. We can't have the world thinking that America's space program is vulnerable to an open homicide."

I thought it through. "So you want me to get the dirt on Taffe, in order for the Mercury Project to stay lily white."

"We want a discrete investigation that gets to the truth," Kirkman said, just like he'd learned it in the movies.

Scott double-teamed me. "Just read the file and keep it to yourself. Don't go around telling anyone anything, until you've reported back to us."

Obviously, the military had its own agenda about this case and these guys wanted me to become a cog in a bureaucratic machine. *Just wait until I get a hold of Walt.* But until then…

Off I go, I thought, *into the wild blue yonder…"*

CHAPTER 14

Climbing high into the sun…

Where, I figured we'd all crash and burn with very little effort once I got back to LA and gave my client a piece of my shaken mind.

I was fuming mad. Indeed, too much was going on behind my back and below my belt. People were getting hurt. I was determined to drop the case, unless someone started giving me good answers, and that would be that.

And then, as I steered my Kaiser back off the base, I saw Gordo's *Star Lady*.

She was long and black and sleek as a shark. She was tucked up under the comforting right wing of a massive B-52 bomber, her short fin wings gleaming in the hot California sunlight.

When I was a kid, I'd had a plastic model of my brother's plane, an F4F Wildcat that I'd hold aloft in my outstretched arm to zoom and swirl into deadly battle. Now, I would have crushed that toy under foot and kicked it into the trashbin, in exchange for fifteen minutes with the elegant beauty on the runway before me.

The photographs of her in Scott and Kirkman's offices didn't do her justice. She was one hell of a classy spaceship.

Somebody said, "Wow." It was me. How could a man who was about to sail into the blue yonder with her, possibly think of ending his own life? I shook my head. Crazy.

⌘

I drove south through Lancaster, Palmdale, and the afternoon heat. The car phone hissed and crackled at me when I tried to reach Norman. Stopping at a Howard Johnson's, I ate a hot roast beef sandwich and a slice of peach pie. Over coffee, I opened the folder and began to read.

Albert Francis Taffe, a captain in the United States Air Force, was born March 11, 1926 in Stone Mountain, Georgia. He is, or was, five foot nine inches tall, 165 pounds and single. His hometown was Dayton, Ohio, where he and his mother, Mrs. Daisy Taffe, owned a small farm. His mother was now residing there. His father, the late Colonel James Taffe, was retired from the air force in 1951 and died in Columbus, Ohio, in November 1955.

Taffe attended primary and secondary schools in Dayton. He entered the Marine Corps in 1945 after his graduation from high school. He attended the Naval Academy Preparatory School for some months and was later a member of the Presidential Honor Guard in Washington until his discharge in August 1946.

He attended the University of Hawaii for three years in Honolulu. While there, he received a commission in the army. He transferred this to the air force and was recalled by that service for extended active duty in 1949 for flight training.

After his training, he was assigned to the Eighty-Sixth Fighter Bomber Group in Munich, Germany, where he flew F-84s and F-86s for four years. While in Munich, he attended the European Extension of the University of Maryland Night School for one year. He attended the Air Force Institute of Technology at Wright-Patterson Air Force Base, Ohio, for two years, where he received a bachelor's degree in aeronautical engineering in August 1956. After his graduation from AFIT, he was assigned to the Air Force Experimental Flight Test School at Edwards Air Force Base. He was graduated from the school in April 1957 and was assigned to duty in the Performance Engineering Branch of the Flight Test Division at Edwards. He participated in the flight testing of experimental fighter aircraft, working as an aeronautical engineer and test pilot.

Taffe had 2,700 hours flying time, 1,400 of which were in jet fighters.

His hobbies were boating and water skiing. His life was the stuff that dreams were made of, and yet perfectly normal for his chosen profession. His psychological evaluation stated that he was stable, adventurous, and slightly lonely. That sounded familiar to me, given that both of us are, or were, bachelors.

I drove back down route 99 to Burbank, thinking and not noticing the traffic or the songs on KFWB-980 on the dial. This case had started out strange and now was positively weird. And that made me think of good old Norman "Weirdo" Weirick again.

I tried the car phone and got him to answer. After we'd talked about the lousy reception in the mountains, I said, "Do me a favor."

"Sure. You can count on me, Mr. Wade."

I gave him Cindy's phone number at the Brown Derby and asked if he could call her and relay the call to me here in the car.

"Sure," he said, but I had my doubts. If all else failed, I could always pull over at a service station and feed dimes into a payphone. A half mile south of Glendale, the car phone buzzed and I picked it up.

"Stan?" Cindy sounded distant and concerned, like she was calling from Mount Everest.

"Hi, kiddo. I was wondering if you know if I have any messages."

"Wait a sec. I have them right here." There was a sound like surf coming in. "Boy, are you ever popular today."

"Really?"

"Yes, really. Let's see. Some guy named Mickey called to apologize. He said that he wished you no harm."

I couldn't decide if that was good or bad.

"And Highway Patrol Sergeant Williams called to tell you to 'watch your step.'"

A brown Chevy station wagon with Indiana plates cut me off. There were two kids in the back licking ice cream cones. Stickers for the Grand Canyon, Petrified Forest, and Disneyland decorated the lower portion of the rear window.

"Lex called with an address for the boat in Redondo Beach."

I pulled to the side of the road and stopped to write the address into my notebook.

"That about it?" I asked coming back onto the freeway to swing west on Route 66. A green Dodge had the right-of-way and wouldn't let me in. I hated the traffic in LA and probably the whole world.

"Well, no," Cynthia said. The phone cleared its throat in my ear. "You got a really creepy message from some guy. All he said was, 'You've been lucky so far. Now butt out.'"

Dean Martin drove by in the lane next to me, picking his nose. He glanced over and saw me wearing an eye patch, with a telephone receiver cradled on my shoulder. I gave him a big thumbs up. He gave me a finger up and stepped on the accelerator.

"What does that mean, 'butt out'?" Cindy's voice called. "Butt out of what?"

I shrugged and almost lost hold of the receiver. "You got me."

"I don't like the sound of that, Stan. Your job is pure trouble. I know; I was watching *Mike Hammer* on TV last night...."

"It's all right, Cindy. No need to worry. Trouble is my business. I'll be in the office tomorrow and everything will be a-okay."

"Tomorrow's Saturday, Stan. It's the weekend and I'll be home with Jimmy. Did you say a-okay? You sound like you're underwater."

I sighed. "We have a bad connection. Guess I'll catch up with you on Monday. Say 'hi' to Jimmy for me, will you? Hope he's feeling better."

"Oh, he is, Stan, thanks. See you soon. Bye-bye."

"Goodbye. Hey, Norman, are you on the line, still?"

Buzz, spit. "Still here, Mr. Wade. Sounds like the phone is working super a-okay."

"Yeah, listen, pal, I'm going to call you back in a bit. Will you be there over the next hour?"

"Sure. You can count on me."

"Thanks, and yes, this phone is pretty cool. You done good."

"Roger. Wilco. Over and out."

Who the hell would call me to say that I'm lucky and now butt out? It had to be someone who knew I had an office at the Derby. Natch. I searched my memory. There was Lex, Norman, Walt, Suzi—

Could Suzi have told her partner George Swan? We hadn't gotten along very well, but he didn't seem like the type to make threatening phone calls. Of course, it could have been Mickey, since he obviously knew how to reach me at the restaurant and had left that "apology" message, but why would he then call back and live an anonymous warning? That didn't even make good nonsense. Hell, I didn't even know what I was supposed to butt out of. It might not even have anything to do with this astronaut death case, at all.

I rummaged through my memory for a reasonable answer. Suppose that my Driver guy had searched me while I was unconscious and taken a business card from my wallet. Then Troca and the Goatee guy could have gotten the address to my old office in the Farraday Building from the card, but that place had burnt down, so…

Which reminded me. I had a score to settle with Troca for putting the pencil to Suzi, not to mention the damage done to my face.

I'd also given my business card to Kirkman, but again it only had my old address on it, not the one at the

Brown Derby, so it couldn't have been him or Colonel Scott who'd called.

I started to feel a dull throbbing in my head from thinking too hard, or from my injury, or from the smog. I blew my nose for relief and dry-gagged another pain pill. I just couldn't figure it, but in a strange way, I'd expected it. When you're an investigator, things don't always align nicely for some time, if ever. You just have to accept it and deal with it, before it deals with you.

CHAPTER 15

In order to deal with it, I drove slowly through a shaded residential neighborhood and passed Taffe's apartment house. It was a long stucco building set far back from the street. A sign with a phone number and *Furnished Apts For Rent* stood on the lawn next to the imitation flagstone walk.

There was also an elderly gent with a sweaty T-shirt, leaning into a clickity-sounding hand mower, clipping the grass. I called Norman back and gave him some instructions.

I had a LA Dodgers baseball cap stuffed in the glove compartment, but there was no point in trying to wear a disguise, what with this eye patch, so I walked along the sidewalk and called, "Hello, there."

The old guy paused in his pushing to run a handker-chief across his balding head.

"I understand that there's a Captain Albert Taffe who lives here."

He stretched a kink out of his lower back and squint-ed. "He did. Some fellows from the air force came and said that he'd passed away in an accident."

"Yes, I know," I offered my hand and we shook. "Ted Carmady from Warner Brothers. Al was a buddy of mine and I was hoping to move into one of your apart-ments, since he'd said what a nice place you have here."

"Sorry, fella. Nothing available right now."

I checked my brother's watch and saw that I had about two minutes to pull this off. "Oh, well, I under-stand. But how about if I have a look at Al's place just so I know the lay of the land?"

He started to shake his head. "His stuff's still in there, fella."

"Yes, I know. And that's all right. You'd be there with me, of course, and it'd only take a few minutes." I raised an eyebrow and it stung me.

He shifted from one foot to the other. "Well…"

"I'll give you five bucks for your time." I smiled my best smile for a one-eyed man and dug out my wallet.

He nodded, accepting the cash.

We went inside and up a flight of worn-carpet stairs, arriving at apartment D. The old guy already had taken out a master key and paused for only a second to unlock the door. Then he stood back, leaving the door open, and followed me in.

The place was compact and nicely furnished. Maybe I *would* move in here, if I could afford the rent. In the distance, a phone rang, right on schedule, and a young voice downstairs soon bellowed, "Pa, there's a guy on the phone that wants to talk to you right away."

I watched the old guy step back into the hall and yell, "Who is it?"

"Says he's a Mr. Ackerman from the Board of Health, looking for some big insects."

"Damn," Pa said and looked at me wandering around the room. "I'll be right back. Don't mess with anything, fella."

I raised a gentle palm and kept a straight face. "Okay. Thanks again."

Seconds later, I started to search. The place was pretty neat and clean for a bachelor pad. As a military man, Taffe had kept it squared away. The furniture was low and Mediterranean. Modern-art curtains hung ceiling-to-floor. Fat-based lamps. Large TV and hi-fi console with big band LPs. Tan carpet from wall to wall.

In one corner of the room, a desk sat covered with air force manuals and a reel-to-reel tape recorder. There was a cast bronze paperweight shaped like the trylon and parisphere that said, *1939 New York World's Fair*. I remembered that my mother had one like it that my Aunt Flo had sent us. Mom kept it on the top of a low bookcase next to a framed photo of my brother in his Army Air Corp uniform.

I switched the tape recorder to Play and heard faint conversations between a man and a woman. I rewound the six-inch reel and slipped it into my jacket pocket. Continuing through the contents of the desk, I didn't find anything more interesting than paid bills and empty pads of paper. There was a glass paperweight that said *Welcome to Munich, Germany*, an empty ashtray, and an equally empty wastebasket.

I checked my watch again. The bedroom and bathroom were off to my left. The bed hadn't been slept in. The alarm clock looked to be set for 5 a.m. Books next to the bed were by Michener, Updike, and Chandler, including the one with "Red Wind." My opinion of Taffe was improving.

The closet held a couple of neatly pressed spare military uniforms. I was looking for one thing in particular—and there it was on the top of the bedroom dresser.

When we'd viewed Taffe's naked body, I'd noticed that he had suntan lines where his watch and ring had been. When we'd examined the items in his locker, the watch was there, but not the ring. Now, I found it setting there on the dresser with a gold-colored chain running through it. It was his air force graduation ring from Wright-Patterson.

I remembered that, unlike most officers, he was unmarried and that in some parts of the military there was a tradition of using your graduation ring for special purposes. It looked like Taffe had a girlfriend and was planning to get engaged. Probably the dark-haired girl in the photograph given to me by Colonel Scott.

I scanned the bathroom and then went out to the kitchenette at the rear of the apartment. Both rooms were tidy and clean. The Formica counters in the kitchen reflected the dull glow of the overhead light. Chrome toaster, can opener, and percolator. Another empty trash basket.

I was peeking into the cabinets under the sink when the old guy came back. There was some kind of electronic microphone taped to the underside of the sink bowl, but I didn't get a good look at it, because Pa was saying, "You don't have to worry about cockroaches, fella. Like I just told the guy on the phone, we spray for them every two months."

"Good, good." I stood erect. "When do you think the apartment might be available?"

"Well, this being the end of the month, as soon as the government lets me put the captain's property into storage. I think his folks are going to come and get it. So, I guess maybe in about a week."

We walked together back toward the hallway. I asked the question he'd been waiting for: "How much is the rent?"

"Seventy-five dollars a month, including the furniture and color TV."

"Sounds good. Do you need a down payment to hold it for me?"

"Always like money," he said as we stepped back outside into the evening's gathering twilight.

I started for my wallet. "Oh geez, I don't have more than a couple of dollars on me now and I need gas. Let me get back to you."

He didn't seem too disappointed, so I pressed my luck. "Al had a girlfriend. Here, I've got a picture of her." I took the photo from my shirt pocket. "Have you seen her here before?"

He looked at the face of the dark-haired girl and said, "Maybe. Can't rightly tell. Now let me ask you one. What happened to your head?"

I sighed. This again.

∽∾∽

"And get that light out of my eye, before you blind me completely."

Norman was wearing one of those round, illuminated mirror headbands that I'd seen on doctors. "Oh, wow. You've been hurt. How are you feeling?"

"Fit as a fiddle and ready for love," I told him.

"I could jump over the moon up above," he answered.

Norman never ceased to amaze me.

"If you don't mind my saying so, Mr. Wade, we

sound like two spies giving each other the call sign. And you look like Bazooka Joe from the bubble gum wrapper cartoons, with that eye piece."

"I thought it made me look extinguished." I discovered that you could not wink wearing an eye patch.

"Or like the line in the song from *77 Sunset Strip*: '…including a pirate eye,'" he snorted, nearly collapsing and losing his glasses.

I laughed too, but Norman never ceased to alarm me.

It was after hours again and we had the empty TV repair shop to ourselves to shoot the bull and, I hoped, inspect the evidence.

"However…" he said.

I waited. Nothing. "However, what?"

He blinked at me through thick lenses. "What were we talking about?"

"Nothing, I guess," I said. *Maybe I should get him examined by a head doctor.* "Okay, well, thanks for making that phone call for me 'Mr. Ackerman.' I owe you one. It gave me enough time to search and find this tape that I want you to play."

He came back to me and brightened. "So, does that mean you'll do some investigating work for me sometime?"

"Sure, Norm. Happy to. Just as soon as I'm free."

"I think Mr. Melmuth is a commie."

I knew that Norman had a frequent suspicion of communists under his bed and elsewhere, but to his latest accusation, I drew a complete blank. "Melmuth? I don't know any—"

"You're standing in his electronics repair store. Claude Melmuth, my boss. I overheard him talking to a guy in here yesterday about the P.A.R.T.Y. I could end up involved in some sort of conspiracy, Mr. Wade. Promise me that you'll look into it, as soon as you can."

I decided that there was no use arguing. "Right, Norman. I'll look into it right away. Now, do you think we can we hear what's on this tape?"

He nodded and took the six-inch reel, holding it up to the light. "Acetate."

I shrugged and we journeyed deeper into the dark and mysterious workroom in the back of the shop.

"Oh," I said, "there was a listening device taped beneath kitchen sink of the apartment where I found the tape. Since the place was bugged, this tape might contain—"

He turned back to me. "Where was it again?"

"In the cabinet under the sink in the kitchen."

He turned away and then slowly turned back to me. "That doesn't make any sense, Mr. Wade. A microphone inside a closed kitchen cabinet wouldn't be able to pick up clear sounds from the rest of the house. Maybe not even from the kitchen, itself."

He had a good point. While he queued up the reel on an enormous tape deck, I picked up a copy of *Mad Magazine* that was lying on a workbench. The cover said, *The*

End of Mad, and when I opened the magazine, I saw that it was printed backward and upside down, so the front was the back, the beginning was the end. Very amusing. Just like my world lately.

Norm turned on the machine and we listened to muted voices for a few seconds, while the strong odors of fried grease and onions floated up at me from a crumpled Jack-in-the-Box carton next to the tape player.

"That's love talk," Norm said. "She's telling him how much she loves him."

"Can you turn up the sound, so I can hear better?"

He stood hunched over the deck and turned a dial. "I think they're going to do it."

The voices on the tape filled the air of the repair shop's back room. A man said, "Let's go in the bedroom and get comfortable." Then, an accented female voice: "Wait, Albert dear. As much as I want you again, I need to confess something."

Norman and I both leaned closer to the rotating reels. He whispered, "I think she's French."

"You know that I love you, but you are not the only man I've been with, no."

"Listen, baby, I don't care anything about your past, as long as you're mine now."

"Yes, Albert, but I don't want to hurt you. If we marry, will it ruin your pilot career?"

"Nothing to worry your sweet little head over. Now come on. Let's go."

There was the sound of rustling cloth and a quiet moan, then, "Stop, please." She sounded a little out of breath. "I have an early call at the studio tomorrow morning."

"Are you kidding?"

"No, dear. There will be time for us soon enough. You'll see."

"Ah, Julie, don't be like that—"

"Let's go out and have dinner like we planned, yes? Then we can be together later for the entire weekend. I'm so looking forward to it, n'est pas?"

"Yep. She's French," Norm said.

The two voices argued for another minute and finally left to the sound of a closing door. After that, the tape just hissed, until Norman shut it off. "This detective business is exciting," he said. "You know, some of the studios are starting to use magnetic tape like this to record complete episodes of TV shows. I'll bet I could make something like that into a security camera for you."

"Detective work is trickier than you think, Norm." I gestured to my head. "Look at what happened to me."

"Ah, I bet I could do it. It's merely deductive logic, like with Sherlock Holmes."

"You think so, huh? Well, just remember that when you've eliminated the possible and the impossible, you probably still don't know what is going on. Wade's law."

He laughed. "Okay, Mr. Wade. Want to see the electric smoke detector I'm working on?"

*e*oe*o*

I knew Mickey Cohen had tried to apologize, but I decided to keep on playing it safe. So I headed back to the Georgian hotel, rather than go all the way down to Redondo Beach where Lex had anchored the boat.

On the drive back, I tried to process all the new information I'd assembled. More than anything else, I was curious about this French girl, Julie, who apparently worked at one of the studios. Once in my hotel room, I placed a call to Walt, thinking, among other things, that he might be able to give me a lead on her. Besides, it was way past the time that we should have talked and I had a bone to pick with him.

Again, there was no answer at the private number he had given me. Great.

To kill time, I took my eye patch off and gave my face a full inspection in the bathroom mirror. I had a hell of a shiner on my left side, but the swelling was completely gone now. The stitches made me think of a shrunken head. I worked my jaw around and experimented with clenching my teeth. There was very little pain, which was a good thing, since I was running low on pills to combat it.

I placed my hand over my right eye and tried to see clearly through my left. The color was there, but the detail was still fuzzy. I blinked, winced, and shook my weary noggin to try to improve the view. It stayed fuzzy.

I went back into the bedroom and tried calling Walt's number again. This time, he picked up after the third ring. I explained that I had information that shouldn't be shared over the phone and that I needed to see him right away. He seemed a little standoffish at my insistence, but finally consented to meet with me tomorrow at the last place I would have expected. "I'm sorry, Walt," I said. "I thought you said Pacific Ocean Park."

"I did, Stan," he answered. "I'll arrange to be there for you in the morning around 10:30 in front of the Flight to Mars ride."

I was tired of being confused. "But POP is an amusement park out at the ocean and you don't own it."

"I know. That's why I'll be dressed as a cowboy. Good night."

I was just plain tired.

CHAPTER 16

ubbles and giant seahorses rotated at the entrance of Pacific Ocean Park, while a mild, sea breeze ruffled my hair. I had woken up at 7 a.m. and taken my time showering, shaving with a hotel razor, and cleaning my .38 with a kit that I kept in the Kaiser's glove box. From a pay phone in the lobby, I'd called long distance to the Palmdale hospital to check on Suzi's condition. A nurse on her floor took the call and told me that she was still asleep, but recovering as well as could be expected.

I'd splurged on eggs Benedict in the hotel restaurant and read the morning paper. The Dalai Lama had fled to India to escape the Red Chinese. Elvis Presley was still in the army and had "no way of telling if my fame is fading." Perry Como had signed a twenty-five- million-dollar two-year contract, the largest in TV history. Dick Tracy was under the ocean. Buz Sawyer was in Hong Kong. Superman was fighting some guy called Metallo. Flash Gordon was fighting some sort of cat people. A new comic, *Sky Masters*, had test pilots experiencing the weightlessness of outer space. Heroes all, but when I was growing up, the one I liked the best was a guy in a dark suit, gloves, and mask.

On the way to POP, I wondered whatever happened to The Spirit as I drove through sunny Santa Monica, past a couple of kids gyrating like Elvis with their hula-hoops and a drive-in theater showing a double bill of *Giant Behemoth* and *First Man Into Space*. It wasn't just Norman who was nuts for this science fiction stuff. It seemed to me that the whole country was slowly going space happy.

This was true even here at Pacific Ocean Park, with the space station feel at the entrance, the Ocean Skyway bubble cars, and the ever-popular twin double ferris wheels, dubbed the Space Wheel ride. I bought a Pay One Price ticket and wandered through the crowd of kids in Keds and tourists in gaudy Bermuda shorts. The rumbling clatter of the Sea Serpent roller coaster was punctuated by the squeals and shrieks of its passengers.

As I rounded the Whirlybird ride and walked past the red and yellow Diving Bells bobbing up from the bottom of an enormous tank of seawater, I spotted a tall man in a tan cowboy hat and open-neck shirt with a loose rawhide tie. He had a trim beard and mirrored aviator sunglasses. He watched the diving bells consume happy park patrons and sink them beneath the surface of the giant tank. Then he looked at me and said in a western drawl, "That thing is dangerous." Two beefy guys with butch haircuts and Botany 500 dark suits stood a few steps away from us.

"Howdy, Walt," I said.

"Meeker. Billy Joe Meeker." He pumped my hand. "Oil man from Dallas. Let's walk."

We strolled past the Flight to Mars ride and took in the mini-cars of the Union 76 Ocean Highway. I heard the roar of a crowd when we neared the seal and dolphin show at the Sea Circus. Walt stepped in a wad of pink cotton candy and one of the beefy guys stooped to wipe it off with a handkerchief. Happy music played from speakers throughout the park—I think it was Lawrence Welk—but nobody in our party spoke until I asked, "Why are you in the cowboy get up?"

"Under cover. Checking out the competition. And stop looking at me in that way. You'll draw attention."

I shrugged. "In that case, I think you're in for trouble. Competitively speaking, this place is awesome."

"You know," he said, "you didn't have to come here like that, wearing a patch on your head as a disguise. I already know you're a private eye."

"It's not a disguise. I got this from a friend in the Outfit," I said and began to brief him on all that had happened since last Tuesday. "So, it looks to me like the

Mob owns both Reliance Management and the protestors," I concluded as we went past the Flying Dutchman ride. "They used the threat of the protestors to try to secure valuable government contracts for Reliance."

Walt kept his head and voice low. "Thanks, Stan. I'll have someone look into stopping them, but you don't really think the Mob had Taffe killed, do you?"

We walked past Emmitt Kelley and the sad clown gave Walt a long, long stare.

"At times, I'm not sure what I think," I answered. "The men at Edwards are concerned about protecting their image. They'd like me to find proof that Taffe was depressed or despondent, in order for the overall Mercury Project to have a clean bill of health."

Walt scratched at the underside of his beard. "That doesn't surprise me."

"Yes, but at the same time, someone still wants to get dirt on the project and possibly wreak it. I found a listening bug in Taffe's apartment that indicates someone is after classified information from our flyboys in the space race."

"That sounds like the Soviets," Walt said and gestured to one of the beefy guys, telling him, "Start a sweep of each candidate's home for listening devices." The guy glanced at me and nodded, stepping back behind us to be with his brother.

I stopped walking. "Wait a damn minute. Those guys aren't your guards, they're feds."

"I wish you hadn't put it so bluntly," he said, walking back to me. "I appeal to your professional sense of honor, Stan, to keep this whole thing discreet. A good man is dead," he said quietly under the din and joy of the park. "An important man. And the nation needs to know why. There's more at stake here than you know, but you've done some exceptional work for me in the past and I appeal to you now to not ask the wrong questions."

We looked at each other for a moment—him with his reflective glasses and me with one good eye.

"I think I'll just cash in my chips and go home, if you don't mind."

"I'll triple your fee."

"Dammit, it's not the money I'm after. I resent being left out of the loop. What the hell is your deal with all this? Tell me the whole thing now, or I walk."

"All right. Come with me."

We went around the side of a California Orange Juice stand and got in line for the Skyway ride. The beefy guys continued to follow and Walt dropped back into character while we were in the crowd. "This here ride looks dangerous to me, with folks getting into them little dangling balls bouncing along a tiny wire out over the ocean." An overweight woman in a floppy sun hat turned around and gave him a dirty look. "I hear tell that they're putting in a much safer monorail ride over at Disneyland."

She ignored him.

As we showed our day passes and climbed into the bobbing, bubble car, the door clamped shut and we lifted off, leaving the beefy boys behind.

Walt switched to his normal voice and scratched his neck. "Damn, this thing itches."

"That's it. I'm dropping the case."

"Now hear me out," he said as the plexiglass and metal bubble car began to jiggle along its cable. "I needed to talk to you without the rent-a-clowns overhearing us." He leaned toward me as we swung out over the Pacific on our way to Mystery Island. "Listen carefully, Stan. We don't have much time."

I began to be concerned, and not just about the ride. "Are you in some kind of danger?"

"Not exactly. Not now, anyway. But we have to talk before this nauseating ride gets back. Ask me anything you want and I give you straight answers."

"Okay. First, those guys back there are FBI, right? And you're involved in some sort of government operation."

He kept scratching at his fake whiskers. "I wouldn't wish this on Castro."

"What?"

"Never mind," he said, slipping off the mirrored glasses. "Yes, just prior to World War II, the FBI recruited me to keep a close eye on some people here in Hollywood. I did that and a few years later became what's called a Special Agent in Charge, meaning that I have a few other people reporting to me, who are involved in the Central Intelligence Agency."

I mulled it over. "The CIA?"

"A subsidiary branch, yes."

"That's what I figured. And those two goons back there aren't so much protecting you as they're keeping an eye on you."

"Sometimes we get caught in our own web, I'm afraid. And that, Stan, is why I need your help. There's a foreign government that is all over me on this and I need you to function as an independent operator."

"Just wait," I said. "Let me think."

He lit a cigarette while I tried to sort it out.

The Skyway ride swung around the farthest pole. My world tilted slightly off center over the blue ocean and came back into alignment above the suspension bridge of the park's man-made jungle.

"We're running out of time," Walt said. "There's a lot going on right now at the agency and there's a presidential election coming up next year. Believe me, Stan, I need someone who I know is clean. Someone I can trust."

I was still torn. Trust was certainly the key point in all of this. I wondered who exactly Stanley D. Wade could trust. The Mob? The military? The commies? None of the above? A good investigator would be able to figure it out. A good detective would rise to the challenge and be neither tarnished nor afraid. A patient, methodical man would go down these mean streets—

The hell with it. I took the photo from my shirt pocket and handed it to him.

He studied it. "It looks like Juliette DeLibre, the French actress that we considered using at Universal for *The Shaggy Dog*."

"Are you serious?"

"Yes, it's going to be my first live comedy."

"No, I mean do you seriously know her?"

"Yes, I think she's over at CBS now, working on a television show there."

"I'm pretty sure that she's also Taffe's girlfriend."

He stepped on his cigarette butt. "Interesting. So, does that mean that you'll follow up and keep me posted? The tripe fee offer was no joke."

The bubble ride bumped back to the start and the door clanged open.

"Sounds charming," I said. "I'll get back to you, Billy Joe."

"Why that'd be right kind of you, pardner," he said, putting his shiny shades back on and dropping into character. The Beef Brothers fell into step behind us. I thought they looked steamed and not just from the southern climate.

"You know what will kill this whole amusement park eventually?" I asked as we strolled past Davy Jones Locker.

"Greedy bankers?" he said.

"Rust from the sea air."

He liked that.

I hung back, while Walt and the boys left the park together, and watched them in the reflection of one of the fun house mirrors until they were an inch tall. Then I started watching a bunch of kids scamper past the cascading wall of water outside Neptune's Kingdom. These youngsters would be adults in ten or fifteen years. I wondered what their world would be like, say, in 1969 to 1974. A lot simpler and safer than now, I hoped. But, somehow…

CHAPTER 17

The slip at Redondo Beach wasn't much and the dock looked like it had been there since the 1930s, unpainted and un-patched. The old cabin cruiser was the largest boat in the water both in breadth and beam.

"Well, if it isn't Sammy Davis Jr.," Lex called as I came aboard. Somewhere in the background I could hear a female voice on the radio singing "Come On A My House."

"Stop with the eye jokes, will you?"

"Well, at least I didn't call ya Popeye."

It was a beautiful day and the sun felt good on my head and shoulders. Lex and I stood on the fantail with a couple of visiting gulls and discussed our fates, or more correctly our pasts and our likely futures. The gulls couldn't have cared less.

Lex was wearing a blue print blouse, cut-offs, and sandals. "So, what does it mean: 'You've been lucky, now butt out'?"

I looked out at the endless ocean and thought of the chain of death and violence that had started up and at least momentarily paused. I thought about the risks I'd taken and the surprises I'd encountered.

"I don't know what it means, exactly, but I also got a message from the Mob and that one sounded like they were sorry for trying to blow up the ship. So, go figure."

You're not thinking that it's safe to go back to Lagoon del Rey, are you?"

"No. I'm not dumb enough to fall for that, but Mickey Cohen's been having trouble keeping his dwarfs under control lately. I guess it'd be best if we hung out here for a while yet."

"Damn straight."

The gulls bobbed their heads in agreement.

"I feel like I'm skidding backward," I told Lex. "But I've decided not to give up. Not to quit. I owe Suzi that much and I owe you—"

"And, you owe the chief."

"—and I owe myself to see things through."

"And you owe your client, if not your country, squirrel."

"Maybe. I'm not sure about the country." I shook

myself, to get out of the mood indigo, and dug out the last cigarette in my pack of Luckys. Since my sinuses were clear today, I wondered again why I kept irritating them by smoking.

Here was something I could definitely quit—again. I crumpled up the pack and threw it overboard. The gulls watched, but were too smart to go for it. "Any beer left in the cooler?"

"No beer today," Lex smiled. "We've got this instead." She held up a half-full bottle of Jamison's, pulled the cork with her teeth, and took a deep swig. *Show off.*

"Not now, thanks. Too early for the hard stuff."

She shrugged. "Five o'clock somewhere in the wide world." A tiny splash of amber spilled from the bottle's open neck. The radio switched to playing "How High the Moon?"

"I came here to check on things with you and the boat," I said, "but now I think I also need your help the case."

She pounded the cork back into the bottle with the flat of her hand. "Like what?"

"Do you think your son can get us into CBS this afternoon?"

Lex ruffled her short hair and spit over the side. "Alex is still a Junior Exec over at Television City and can get his mom in any time she asks. What do you need?"

I explained about Taffe's supposed girlfriend and

how Walt had identified her as an actress from France, currently working at CBS.

"Okay," she said. "I can get you in, but we need to stop off at my place first, so I can change clothes."

We secured the boat and piled into my car. I drove up the Pacific Coast Highway behind a beat-up station wagon with surfboards sticking out the back. During the drive, we stopped for tutti-frutti ice cream and Lex played with Norm's car phone, until we reached the beach house. She had a small apartment above the garage where she lived *gratis* for housesitting the place for a VP at one of the studios.

While she changed clothes, I ran across the PCH to a tourist-trap store to buy a couple rolls of film for the Polaroid camera that I kept in the Kaiser's trunk. The kid behind the counter asked the question about what happened to my head and I told him that I'd slipped and walked into the door of the shower. I was getting creative about the whole thing now.

When I got back, Lex was waiting in a crisp sky-blue skirt and blouse, her hair brushed back and clipped neatly into place. "I called Mr. Bigshot Alex Church," she said, sliding back into the passenger seat, "and let him know we were coming."

"So, he didn't like the name Iglesia and changed it to Church, huh?"

"I don't get to see him as much as I used to when he was just starting out in the business." She tapped a fingernail experimentally against the plastic sheet that covered the passenger-side window. "Guess, ya gotta do stuff like that in order to make it in Hollywood. His old man woulda strangled him for it."

I left that alone and, minutes later, pulled off Beverly Boulevard at Fairfax and into the lot at CBS Television City.

We parked on the east side of the monster-sized building in the lot near a helicopter pad. Gilmore Field Stadium used to stand here, hosting family-friendly baseball games, before being torn down last year. The smog was heavy in this part of the city, and it made my eyes, both good and bad, water. I sneezed three times hard, increasing the already sharp pain in my head. Lex blessed me each time.

I loaded film into the Polaroid and we walked past a loading dock to the front of Television City complex. Once inside the massive main building, we were conducted by a uniformed page to the Craft Shop where Alex Church managed team of technicians who maintained the studio cameras.

The lean executive was about my age and had his mother's flint-chip eyes. He wore a clean, mechanic's jumpsuit and crew-cut, sandy hair.

"Mom, can't you see that I'm working here? You've got to—And, you—" He turned to me and paused. "What happened to your…"

"Head? I'm breaking in a new one."

He didn't get it, instead launching back into, "Stop dragging her into these things. She's not a PI. She could get seriously injured."

I had only met Alex once before while on a case at UCLA and knew that he was tight as a tennis racket and sharp as a pair of scissors. He, in turn, thought I was dumb as a paperweight.

"It's all right, Alex," I said. "We're visiting, just like tourists, okay?" Rock breaks scissors. I flashed him Juliette's photo. "We're looking for this woman."

To his credit, he didn't say a word about my eye patch. "How am I supposed to—You're in here to use me for your crappy little—Wait, I just saw her over in Studio 33."

A thin, tanned gent in a tailored suit came up the stairs from the basement as we walked down a long hall. "Is that the *House Party* man, Art Linkletter?" Lex whispered.

"Yes, Mom," Alex said. "The dressing rooms are downstairs."

I heard a jazz combo playing as we continued down the hall past a recording studio. Through the large double-paned window, I could see Miles Davis recording in Studio 61 with that new sax player, Dave Brubeck. I wanted to pause and listen to the beat, but Mr. Church urged us on through the swinging doors of Studio 33.

It was a high-ceilinged cavern with rows of theater seats slanting down in a cascade to a brightly lighted stage at the far end. Huge air-conditioning units hung from the ceiling next to banks of lights to bleed off the generated heat. Wide platforms on either side of the stage provided maneuvering space for the television cameras. A collection of men were seated around a table in the middle of the stage, talking, arguing, and smoking. A few folks sat in the audience.

Alex gazed around. "I don't see her. Come on. We can…Let's ask."

We walked down the carpeted aisle. Lex pointed up at the stage and gasped. "Is that Kookie?"

Alex hushed her.

"Yes, I hear that he just walked off 77 at Warners," I said.

They both looked at me, perplexed.

"What? I read the trades."

"He's meeting with Jack about appearing on his show," Alex said.

Jack, I knew, was Jack Benny, the man with the open-neck polo shirt, sport coat, glasses, and cigar. He rehearsed and recorded his show here in Studio 33 to be broadcast Sunday nights. As my little group neared the stage, Ed "Kookie" Byrnes held Jack's attention and was the epitome of "cool" in a tan Palm Beach jacket with pale blue shirt, navy tie, and matching beltless Jay-mar slacks.

"He's gorgeous," Lex said.

"Mom…" Alex said,

Lex nudged me with an elbow. "Get a picture of him."

I tried to open the camera, but the latch was stuck. I must have jammed it when I'd loaded the film. While the men in front of us continued to shuffle pages and read lines, various people crossed the stage, calling to one another and checking things off on clipboards. I stopped one guy coming down the aisle, wearing a set of headphones with the wire and plug dangling, and asked about Juliette DeLibre. He gave me a blank stare, until I showed him the photo. Then he said, "Oh, yeah. I think that broad was over at MGM working on the new Philip Marlowe TV show for ABC."

"Alex, can we meet Kookie?" Lex whispered.

I said to the sound guy, "Wait, there's a Marlowe television show in the works?"

"Excuse me, gentlemen," Alex called out, and the crowd on the stage looked in our direction.

"Yeah," the sound guy said. "But it won't last long. Not with that Phil Carey starring in it."

"We're looking for Juliette DeLibre," Alex called up to the stage.

Jack Benny turned his head to the left and right. "That's funny. She was just here a minute ago."

Lex waved. "Hiya, Kookie."

A technician came dashing toward us. "Mr. Church, we're having a problem with one of the RCA TK-41s. It's smoking again."

"Shit." Alex turned and ran to the side of the studio, out an exit, like Bugs Bunny.

A chestnut-haired young woman in a white outfit entered from stage left. I moved up the stairs to meet her. "Juliette?"

"*Oui?*"

She held a hand above her face to see who had called. Soft makeup couldn't hide her freckles from the bright studio lights, nor her dazzling hazel eyes.

Lex moved up the steps behind me. "Mr. Benny, I've got a great idea how to improve your show."

Jack looked around some more, trying to figure out what was going on, especially between Juliette and me. Finally, he locked onto the gravel-voiced woman who had addressed him.

"Lookit," he said, standing. "I'd love to hear your suggestion, but I'm late for a dentist's appointment that I've been looking forward to for three weeks. Can we have some security in here?"

I urgently addressed Juliette. "I have a tape with your voice on it. It's from Albert Taffe's apartment."

The dazzle widened in her eyes, while a short guy with slicked-back hair, who looked like a midget Mickey Cohen, if such a thing were possible, stepped out from the crowd behind Jack and headed directly for us, carrying a guitar by the neck.

I jiggled the camera and handed it to Lex. "See if you can get this to work."

"Wait a minute, Remley," Jack said. "Stay out of it. Let security handle it."

Juliette smiled weakly. "My brother wanted me to spend time with the captain, yes?"

"Get a picture of her," I said to Lex.

Lex ignored me. "You guys aren't listening—"

Three security cops rushed down the aisle. Things were going from bad to forget it.

Remley glared at me with chocolate-brown eyes and seized my elbow. "Hey, masked man, you want to give Mr. Benny a little air?"

"Wait a minute, Fred," Jack said. "Leave them alone."

The uniformed cops were now assembled around us.

"Wait a minute—" Jack said,

Lex pushed in toward Remley. "Is this guy giving you trouble, Stan?" She wound up to take an open-hand swing at his face.

I saw a way to end the chaos and yelled, "Wait a damn minute!"

Everyone froze, until somebody said, "Get 'em out of here!"

The security guys moved in, as Jack said, "Hey— that's my line."

One of the guards grabbed Lex from behind.

"Cut that out, buster," she hollered.

"They're doing my entire act," Jack complained, as we were being herded away back up the aisle.

Five minutes later, we were back in my sun-baked Kaiser Manhattan.

"Crap. We didn't get a picture of *nobody*," Lex said. She banged the Polaroid on the dashboard and the film flipped out.

There wasn't enough Darvon in the world to cover my pain.

CHAPTER 18

On the way back to the boat, I stopped in at my cubby-hole office in the Brown Derby. It was after 5:30, late on a Saturday afternoon, and the place was already hopping. The restaurant had no race restrictions, thus Lena Horne was dining with Eartha Kitt. At another table, Mario Lanza was eating with a guy who looked like Jascha Heifetz. It must have been "musician's night" here at the Derby, or maybe they were all going to appear together later at the Hollywood Bowl.

I found no important mail on the floor of my office, but there was a note from Carlos that told me of a package waiting on Cynthia's desk. I located the small box that had arrived earlier in the day by special delivery from Walt. My client had been a busy cowboy.

Inside the package were fuzzy, muddy-looking photostats of pages from the passports of Juliette and Thomas Fayard. Juliette's picture was an unglamorous shot of my French actress. Apparently, DeLibre was a stage name. The other photo was a similar straight-on view of my goateed beatnik.

I resisted the urge to give a low whistle and stuffed the photos and accompanying pages of information into the inside breast pocket of my jacket next to my pen and pad. There was also a note from Walt, saying that I had a dinner date with Juliette set for that evening to discuss "possible additional scenes to be shot and added to *The Shaggy Dog.*"

I was to meet her at 8 p.m. at Andre's of Beverly Hills. Fitzy, rancy place, indeed.

When I got back to my car, I found Lex dozing, probably from the heat and the Irish whiskey. I escorted her back to her garage-top apartment and continued on to the *Cervantes II* in order to clean up and dress for dinner.

My face was just about back to its normal handsome color, but the lack of haircut and the itching stitches over my left eye made me look like Frankenstein's brother. I went, "Grrr…" In the mirror. "Smoke. Bad." Then I put the eye patch back into place and went "Ahrrr, matey…"

It was nearing 7 p.m. when the distinctive smell of seaweed carried up from the in-coming tide, and I hopped back in the Kaiser, heading for a quick stop at the A-1 Electronics shop.

✄✎✄✎

"Okay. I got the camera fixed," Norman said, finishing off a Mars bar. "Plus I added an infra-red light source attachment and a roll of special film, so you can take pictures in the dark. Neato, huh?"

"Won't the flash give me away?"

"The human eye can't see light from the infra-red spectrum. And I think I've worked out a way to put a television set in your car, if you like."

"Geez, Norm, isn't there anything you can't get to run in my Kaiser? How about a nuclear reactor or a time machine?"

"Don't be absurd. But…"

I could almost see the wheels spinning in his brain.

"Boy, that must be some exciting case you're on. Wish I could go." His eyes widened. "When you say 'Walt,' are you talking about Walt Kelly who drawls Pogo, or Wally Wood, the comic artist?"

I pointed to the passport photos of Juliette and Thomas Fayard that I had set on the workbench. "Is there any way you can make better copies of these muddy pictures?"

He studied the photostats. "Sorry, Mr. Wade, these are copies of copies and much too grainy for me to improve upon. I'd have to…" He trailed off, lifted his glasses to his forehead, and peered intently at the portraits.

"What?"

"I know this guy." The glasses dropped down into place on his nose. "He's a commie. He was here in the shop the other day, talking to Mr. Melmuth about the American Workers Alliance."

"No offense, Norm, but it seems that you tend to see communists just about everywhere."

"No, no. I'm sure, in this case. There's a meeting Saturday night at midnight on Olympic near Santa Fe Avenue."

"This Saturday? Today is Saturday. Norm, that's to-night."

He glanced at an insurance calendar with a Maxfield Perish print. "So it is."

It suddenly struck me that my goateed guy, Fayard, might not be so much a mob-related protestor, as he was part of Walt's supposed Soviet threat. I looked up and damned if I didn't find an exposed light bulb hanging from a cord above my head.

"Do you want me to put a two-way radio into your watch?" Norman asked.

My mind came back home. "Uh, do you mean like Dick Tracy? What? You can actually do that?"

"Yeah, that's where I got the idea. I really like those detective stories. I'm even thinking of adding a private eye to the novel I'm writing. And I've got more chapters for your to read when you have the time."

I couldn't resist patting him on the back. "Soon, Norman, soon. And the thing about the watch-radio sounds good, provided you can get it to work better than the car phone. On the other hand, you know that this watch is very important to me. It's sort of a family heirloom, Norm. I got it from my brother and he's—"

"Okay, I get it. I get it. Some other time then, huh?" I could tell he was disappointed. "Here, you might need this." He handed me a black plastic box the size of a deck of cards. It had a single button on one side.

"What does it do? Nothing happens when I push the button." I pressed it several times to prove my point.

"It would if you were near the right television set or garage door."

I felt my leg being stretched. "Very funny." I tossed the box onto a workbench. "Thanks anyway. Not interested."

"Not even remotely?" He snickered at his new joke and I let him enjoy it.

"Oh-kay. I think that's just about wraps up this evening's entertainment. Thanks, again, Norm. You're a Godsend."

He smiled, raised his eyebrows, and pointed upward. "Keep watching the skies."

I reminded myself of "joyful participation" and took off with the modified Polaroid camera before the little green men with nets could show up.

∽∾∽

I drove south on Sepulveda, past the LA Airport and endless stretches of oil fields, where pumps seesawed up and down like those bird-toys that appeared to drink water. I nosed the Kaiser Manhattan west to the beach city of the same name, until I reached Ocean Way and an expensive four-story apartment house. Four miles south of here, the *Cervantes II* lay in a birth at Redondo Beach.

An Otis elevator took me to the penthouse and I did my trick of checking my looks in the mirrored inner door. I confirmed that my appearance was acceptable, under the circumstances, and that my fly was high.

She answered the door on my first chime. Her shining dark hair fell in luscious sheaths at the side of her pert face with those bright hazel eyes. I couldn't think of anything smart to say, except, "You look great."

She reached up and straightened the knot in my tie. "Stop fidgeting."

"Sorry." Her perfume was the sweetest thing I'd smelled in a thousand years.

"No need to apologize," she said. "Shall we go?"

"We shall, indeed."

Twenty minutes later, we were led to a small table in the downstairs room of the pricey American/French/Italian restaurant on Welshire. The waiters of Andre's kept coming and going, totting spaghetti and steaks on big platters and smiling down benignly.

Juliette sat with her hands folded in her lap, studying the bottle of Californian Pinot Noir on the table.

"Go ahead. Take a drink," I said. "It's not as good as your country's wine, but I think you'll like it."

"When will you tell me about the new scenes for the movie, Mr. Wade?" she asked in a clear, musical voice.

Heads turned to look at us. She dropped her gaze to her lap. I tried to seem as ordinary as a light switch.

"Relax," I said. "Call me, Stan."

"*D'accord.*"

"First, I'm going to ask a few questions and you can answer them."

She shrugged and drank some wine. The waiter came and took our orders.

"Tell me first about your relationship with Albert Taffe."

She looked past my left shoulder, gazing into the well of her past. "I wondered if that subject would come up. There is not much to tell," she said slowly. "But still, it is difficult. I hardly know you."

"I think you can trust me."

She finished her wine. I filled her glass again, but she left it on the table. "I am what you call an addict," she said gravely, as though admitting she had some incurable and highly contagious disease. Tears began forming in her eyes.

This was a surprise. Was she trying to impress me with her acting skills? "Take it easy. An addict of what?"

"My brother did it. Oh, I hated him. At first, I thought it wouldn't matter, just a little every now and then, to show I was…well, sophisticated. But then I came to crave it. Truly I could not live without it, and when that happened I would do anything he wished. Anything." She clinched her fist next to the wine bottle, bunching the tablecloth. "What am I going to do?"

I lowered my voice. "Are we talking about marijuana?"

"*Oui*, marijuana. What am I going to do?"

I decided that there was a chance that she might be telling the truth and that I should do something to help her. "Begin by not feeling sorry for yourself," I said harshly. "You're no addict."

She jerked her head back as though I had struck her. "It's easy for you to say."

"Who told you marijuana's a narcotic? It's no more habit-forming than cigarettes or whiskey. It just makes it easier for you to move on to the hard stuff. I smoke a pack of cigarettes a day. I want one now, but I'm not going to."

"Then you should stop smoking altogether," she said flatly, but for the first time there was the slightest hint of a smile in her hazel eyes. "*Comme la dindon froid.*"

"If that means 'cold turkey,' I did just that, earlier today."

She laughed. "Very valiant, but we shall see, no?"

The waiter arrived and displayed our rack of lamb with a flourish, then took it to a nearby serving table to carve. The tender meat oozed juices as the knife bit through it. I certainly was dining on a lot of lamb this season. My expense report to Walt was going to be huge. When the two plates had been set before us, I asked again about Taffe.

Juliette chewed enthusiastically and talked at the same time. I decided that was a good sign. I got the idea that feeling sorry for herself was at least half her problems, but when I looked deeply into her eyes, I could see a genuine pain from something she didn't want to talk about.

"Tell me more about your brother."

"He came over with me from France, when my opportunities here started to blossom. He helps me in the day-to-day activities, allowing me to concentrate on my career."

I slowly rotated my wine glass on the linen tablecloth. "What are his politics?"

"French politics are very complex. We have so many parties, you see? I do not understand it all."

She put down her knife and fork and finished the wine in her glass. "It takes all my energy and concentration to have a career as an actress and to maintain my reputation as a professional. At the end of the day, I am often exhausted. Why all these questions about Thomas?"

I fell back on playing the role Walt had given me. "The studio has its own reputation to consider, and we are constantly looking to improve our image in the public's mind. You seem to fit our wholesome standards, but we need to be sure that there are no relationship that could come back on us. Speaking of which, your relationship with Captain Taffe seemed quite intimate before he died."

"Albert is dead? *Mon Dieu*, how? When?"

"You didn't know? No, of course not. The air force is keeping it quiet." I cleared my throat. "He died only a few days ago, during an apparent training accident. I'm sorry to be the one to tell you."

"Oh, that is so sad." He eyes misted slightly. "I will never see him again. I will never forget him."

"You don't seem too broken up by the news."

"Albert was a dear man, but only one of many, you see. American's are so fortunate and so naive. Yes, we made love, but as a French woman, you must understand that I have different attitudes in these matters than the people of your country."

"And your attitudes about drugs are quite different, as well," I said as we sampled our profitoralls. "Look, I understand, really. You're a nice kid who got mixed up in a situation that got out of control but, believe me, you can't let it take charge of your life."

"Those are just words. I'm a grown woman. I know what I want. What I need." As though to disprove the assertion of her maturity, she began to cry softly.

I gave her my handkerchief. She blew her nose in it hard. I asked for the check and paid it. Then I told her that I'd be in touch about the part in the movie. She sniffed and nodded her appreciation, as we went outside to the Kaiser, which was being viewed with interest by an elderly couple on the sidewalk.

On the drive back to her apartment on Ocean Way in Manhattan Beach, she pretended not to notice the Kaiser's damaged window. I told her that the phone was a direct line to my office and she seemed impressed. We grew quiet for the rest of the drive and at her door, we both said, "Adieu" and kissed each other's cheeks in the French manner before she went inside.

The sweet, young taste of Juliette's face lingered on my mouth. Yes, we Americans *are* fortunate and I'd *been* lucky so far.

It was nearing midnight. I walked with grace to my car, but I wasn't going to butt out.

CHAPTER 19

AWA Meeting. Members ONLY.

The sign was pinned to several posts in the parking lot of a warehouse the size of an airplane hangar near an SPRR freight yard.

This was not a secret meeting of spies, I thought, threading my way among the parked cars and trucks. Rather, it was an open gathering of electricians, carpenters, and gofers—honest workers who yearned for something extra, beyond what the corporate execs were willing to give.

Over the past few years, the Party had quietly made steady inroads among film-industry employees, now that the old studio system was crumbling and television production was expanding. Ordinary guys and a few gals were gathering here tonight in an effort to make their lives a bit better. I was no red-baiter, but it seemed to me that what these people didn't know was that the American Workers Alliance took their contributions and gave back more doubt than honor, more fear than hope.

The moon shone one-quarter full and burnt orange through the smog. I smacked a mosquito that wanted to taste me, totted my Polaroid through the darkness, scanning for a way into the meeting hall. There didn't appear to be any solid security at the main entrance, but I didn't have an invite and didn't know the password, so I poked around the side of the building and found a fire escape to the second floor. Once up top, my way was blocked by a locked door and a set of louvered windows covered with peeling paint. I listened, only hearing the low rumble of general voices in the open hall below.

One of the windows stood open part way. Reaching a hand inside, I released a catch and squeezed through. Inside, I unlatched the door for easy exit and turned to scope out the gantry platform that supported me along the wall above the crowd. Shielded light fixtures dangled from the ceiling, casting a glow on the meeting beneath me, while keeping the upper walkway in shadow. I leaned forward to get a better view of the crowd and perhaps even a photo, when the rickety landing creaked under my weight. A figure moved in the darkness to my right.

If he'd come from my left side where my eye was

patched, I'd have never seen him in time. He carried what looked to be a 20-gauge shotgun. The light from below us haloed the barrel as he eased in my direction. I must have been the shadows, because his eyes were tight and searching in the reflected light.

I hadn't breathed since I'd spotted him and still didn't. I watched him slowly rotate sideways for a better view. He suddenly turned and looked directly at my face.

A sound started coming out of his mouth when I grabbed the shotgun with both hands and pivoted the butt up and into his chin. It sounded like a fastball hitting a Louisville slugger. He teetered for a second and then started to go over backward, but I came in close and pulled his collapsing body into me.

He went loose as a swivel chair while I held him up for a few more seconds and then he started to snore. I lowered him to the deck with one arm and took full control of the scattergun with the other, silently thanking Dave Sharpe again for that year of stunt training at Republic. I extracted the shells from his gun, pocketing them in my jacket, and left the breach-broken weapon in a darkened corner farther down the walkway.

Below my feet, the meeting was just getting started. Well over sixty people mingled in the dusty, smoke-filling hall as I fought back the urge to sneeze. They were still talking among themselves and milling about, when from my unique vantage, I spotted a particularly interesting blonde, stacked like a deck of cards, introduce a white-haired duck in a cream-colored suit. He walked to a table positioned in front of the rows of chairs, raised his hands, and called everyone to be seated, like it was a minstrel show.

The duck spoke for a while, casually, in deep tones and open gestures. Most of the audience seemed to follow his presentation with calm interest. A few looked like they were dozing. "If we all hang together, we won't hang separately" seemed to be tonight's main topic. It was a distorted view of democracy and it was bubbling up all around me.

I kept my good eye on the guy that I'd cold-cocked, while scanning the crowd below for my goateed query, Thomas Fayard. I began to wonder if Norman had been overly paranoid about the whole thing, when the white-haired duck's speech ended to applause and the meeting began to break apart. Then, I saw him.

He had hung back at the rear of the crowd, as if he were shy about being there, but now made his way around the right side of the audience to meet with the duck and shake his hand. They stood together, directly below me, some twenty feet down. I studied the tops of their heads, thinking that this definitely proved the Mob, or at least Fayard, was connected to the local communist cell.

I popped open the camera to get photographic evidence, but the angle was all wrong. Then the duck handed Fayard a set of keys and patted him on the shoulder, like a proud papa. The snoring behind me quieted. I didn't know what that meant, but I didn't like it. Fayard had started walking back to the building's entrance.

I skedaddled out the door and down the fire escape, hoping to catch him in the dim parking lot. After a few seconds, I saw him stepping through a folding door like they had on phone booths. Only this door was on the side of a blocky, pale delivery truck with white sidewall tires and *Cloverleaf Dairies* painted on its side.

∽✤∽

We drove over the Los Angeles River and caught the Santa Ana Freeway going south. I kept back from him in the Kaiser, staying tucked behind the few cars that were on the 101 at this late hour of the night. I checked the radium dial of my brother's watch. It was 1:25 in the morning.

We traveled peacefully at posted speeds, past exits for Montebello and Norwalk and the cutoff for Riverside. We slowed near Anaheim and I began to have a bad feeling about where we were headed. Fifteen minutes after we'd started, the milk truck came off the freeway onto Harbor Boulevard and I knew I was right. His taillights flared as he turned left into the half-filled parking lot of a Magic Kingdom motor lodge. I whizzed on down the road, noticing that he'd pulled up next to a long, dark Caddy.

I'd had been so intent on watching the vehicle in front of me that I hadn't noticed the headlights far in back of me. I told myself that this happened occasionally to the best detectives. *Yeah, sure.* Now what had I stepped into?

❧

I drove farther down the road and switched off my lights, navigating by moonlight and a few neon signs. I turned into the lot of a restaurant that was closed and dark at this late hour and waited, watching the milk truck from behind a stand of some shrubs, before slowly pulling around the building to find an access area that adjoined the motel lot.

I moved forward and the truck came back into view. Its lights were off. Nothing moved. What the hell? I unscrewed the bulb in my dome light and quietly opened the car door. A semi-truck zoomed past on Harbor, doing over sixty, running a red light in the middle of the night. I waited until the sound of its passing faded and then crouched down to glide among the few parked cars that were scattered throughout the lot. I was within ten feet of the dairy truck when I almost kicked an empty beer bottle. I shifted my weight in the other direction, when a voice hissed, "Hold it, my friend."

I hadn't noticed Fayard's accent before. Maybe he'd been hiding it, but I got it now, as he pushed a gun into my side.

Then a guy wearing a sporty hat rose up from behind an Olds. "You hold it yourself, shithead." George Swan stepped into the muted light of an overhead lamppost, pointing what looked to me like a heavyweight .44 Magnum revolver at Fayard. My shirt stuck to my back from sweat.

The eyes in the goateed face next to me ping-ponged to the cop and then back to me and then back to the cop.

"Put it down easy, asshole," George said,

Fayard screwed up his face and I thought I was going to become a perforated Univac punch card. Instead, he slowly bent to place his gun on the blacktop, and I breathed easier.

"Everybody stop and freeze just like you are," another voice commanded from behind the black Caddy.

I was getting lost among all the guns. Simple math told me the score was two to one in their favor.

Fayard began to grin. "Nice one, Troca." He jabbed the barrel of his weapon back into my kidneys. "Put your damn hands back up."

"Hey, George," I called. "Speaking of backup, where's yours?"

Troca looked around, while yanking Swan's firearm from his hand. We all tensed even more, waiting to see if anyone else joined our party.

"You know damn well where she is," George said,

That was correct, I did. But the other guys didn't. We all stood there waiting to see who would pop up next. I couldn't think of anything smart to say. George gave me a look that could have soured all the cream at Cloverleaf Dairies. The gun in my harness leather felt like it would burn through to my chest. Finally, Fayard read my mind and pulled it free, laughing under his breath.

George started to say something, but Troca cut him off. "Shut up. Ain't nobody else coming." He had every-thing under control now. The mobster did his little trick of shifting his shoulders and neck to be more comforta-ble, patted George down, and found his holdout and handcuffs.

Fayard gave me the same treatment and came up empty. "Put the cuffs on 'em," he told Troca. And, once we were linked together, he shoved us through the accor-dion doors of the milk truck and told Troca to drive.

As the truck bumped along, George and I sat on the floor with our backs against a stack of cardboard cartons and wooden crates. The cop's left hand was cuffed to my right. He was still wearing his nifty hat and sour expres-sion. I looked at him with one eye. "I'll bet you and I are leaning against something a lot more powerful than cot-tage cheese."

CHAPTER 20

Like almost everyone else in Southern California under the age of eighty, I had been to Disneyland before and had also read in the newspapers accounts of its current expansion. The original park had its entrance off Harbor with a shopping-center-sized parking lot to the south and administration buildings to the north. The new construction for the monorail, submarine ride, and man-made Matterhorn Mountain was amassing in the northeast quadrant of the original park, just above Tomorrowland.

A high chain-link fence surrounded the erection supply and staging area next to the maintenance buildings. During the day, work gangs parked here and assembled together among the tool sheds and heavy equipment vehicles to enter into the expanding hard-hat park grounds where the new rides would soon operate. During the night, the place was a graveyard.

As Troca drove the milk truck into the construction site, north of the main attractions, I saw through the windows in the passenger-side door a broad metal sign attached high on the fence: Reliance Management Corporation. It wasn't much of a surprise that the company that hoped to gain contracts at Edwards Air Base was the same company building part of the expansion here at the park. But then, why were they trying to take down Disneyland? And why kill an astronaut? I knew Troca was part of the Mob and that the Mob was connected to Reliance, but how did Fayard and the commies fit in? Whatever the answers, Walt's offer to triple my fee wasn't going to be nearly enough compensation to untangle this mess.

Time was, back in the early '50s, communist activities in America were clandestine, consisting of secret meetings and undercover identities. Those days were now behind us, probably because of Russia's recent successes in space. Today, the members of the Party were emboldened to take action, as if there were a ticking-bomb timetable they felt compelled to meet. Perhaps Walt was right, and it had something to do with the presidential election next year. Perhaps it had to do with the phases of the moon.

I didn't presume to understand it, but I knew it when

it hit me between the eyes, and right now my head was reeling.

Fayard and the stiff-necked mobster stood in the cab area of the truck, adjusting their immediate plans now that they had unexpected passengers.

"So if I still do this, your guys will give me protection, right?" Troca said.

"Hey, Troca," I called, "did I get you in trouble with your boss?"

"You prick. Shudup back there."

Just another cheap thug. But a dangerous one.

The milk van pulled up beside an electrical substation and our two hosts got out. Fayard waited just outside the truck, while Troca unlocked the door to the concrete-block building and disappeared inside.

It seemed pretty clear to me that Swan and I were destined to soon be shot and/or blown up with the truck full of explosives. I raised my wrist in front of George's face. "Key?"

He nodded, silently fished one out of his trouser pocket, and unlocked the cuffs. "We're going to take these geniuses on my count of three."

"Hurry it up in there, Frankie," Fayard called out.

Troca must have jimmied a power circuit, because the main access gates began to open, allowing us entrance to the park central without sounding an alarm. The same circuit also must have controlled power to some of the rides, including the new ones still under construction. The submarine voyage and the monorail started to illuminate and glide on their paths.

Our captors came back aboard the delivery van and pulled it farther into the park. Nearby, I could hear the rushing sounds of moving water and a dull hum above our heads as the train slowly began to move along its singlewide rail. Our truck came to a stop again next to the man-made mountain of the Matterhorn that looked like a network of pick-up-sticks gantries and frames.

Down behind our captor's backs, George caught my eye and raised three fingers, then two, then one, and we sprang up in unison from the vehicle's floor. I dove forward into Troca's lower back taking him with me out the open truck door. He slammed to the ground on his knees, cushioning my fall, while I punched him under the right ear. The gun he held spiraled and half-buried itself in a mound of gravel and we both scrambled forward.

I got to it first and rolled, kicking Troca with pleasure and both feet. He went "Ugh" like a reasonable facsimile of Chief Thunderthud. I brought the weapon up and was surprised to see that it was my own .38, but my target was already rushing behind one of the concrete stanchions that supported the monorail ride. I had my gun, but he still had his, so I ducked around a nearby bulldozer and squinted my good eye, trying to catch any movement in the darkness.

A shot popped like a toy balloon a hundred yards or more behind my back and another deeper-sounding report followed. Swan must have been in a gun battle with his opponent, just as I was.

A bullet from Troca wanged off the side of the dozer. I gathered myself for a run.

The shadows shifted on my right and I again heard the low roar of the monorail as it passed overhead. It would be good tactics to take the high ground. I hoped that Troca didn't have the same idea.

Clambering up the side of the bulldozer, I leapt to grasp the top of the support structure. I hung there for a second, listening, then quickly swung a leg over and came to a stand almost eighteen feet above the ground. There was a raised hump running along the center of the skinny platform. I figured that it held a rail that was probably electrified. Not something I wanted to touch, now that the power was switched on.

I crouched down to make myself a smaller target. Bursts of light and snapping reports kept coming from the other side of the man-made mountain, where George still must have been dealing with Fayard. I saw a nearer muzzle flash and heard the simultaneous whine of a bullet streaking past my head from farther down the track. Somehow, Troca had climbed up the onto platform with me and was coming my way. We were trading shots at point blank range. I turned, following the track around a gradual curve into a dark patch of night, where the sound of rushing water grew louder beneath the narrow platform.

I searched in vain for any sort of cover, but except for the foot-high raised rail that guided and empowered the train, the track was bare. From out of the darkness, a faint roar began to advance from Troca's direction. It had to be the monorail train coming toward us at a good ten-miles-per-hour. If he didn't jump, it would reach him before it would reach me, so all I had to do was wait and perhaps he'd run right to me.

The roar increased and I could see him moving forward in the half-light. I looked down and to my right, spotting a mound of sand below. I was preparing to duck and shoot and jump, when Troca turned to face the approaching line of thirty-foot long steel cars. If he thought he could shoot it out with the train, he was nuts. If he thought he could out run the thing now, he was crazy.

"Don't do it!" I yelled and, as I leapt to my sand pile, I saw that he *was* crazy—like a fox.

While I fell to the right side of the train platform, he jumped to the left. I hit the sand and rolled, my gun slipping from my hand into the darkness. I came back up as fast as a jack-in-the-box to hear a loud splash from the opposite side of the rail supports. I pawed the ground for my gun, trying to picture where Troca had gone. At this location in the park, the monorail stretched up over the lagoon that contained the sub ride. Shots from Swan and Fayard continued to sound from farther away, but my concentration centered on the high wall that surrounded the ride from *Twenty-thousand Leagues Under the Sea.*

I took advantage of a patch of shadow as protection and looked down into the inky waters swirling in the submarine pit. Troca was there, lying on his back across the forward portion of one of the ornate subs. From his reclined position on the glowing sea-serpent vessel, he managed to spot me and fired another shot up at my head.

The water around his boat and prone form began to bubble. Compressed air made the wet surface seem to boil. Troca stopped aiming in my direction, did his nervous head and shoulders jerk, and started scanning around the lagoon as his sub began to move. There was something wrong with his right leg. He pulled frantically at his foot which appeared to be trapped in the intricate exterior design of the submarine.

The water came up fast. He was caught on the ride as it began to sink beneath the manufactured waves. He looked up at me and screamed my name again and again, firing his last rounds helplessly into the night sky as the sub pulled him beneath the surface and together they slid into the underwater tunnel that lead to cement mermaids and the airless lost city at the bottom of the Magic Kingdom.

Another shot rang out from George's direction, closer than the ones before. I rushed back to the sand pile, groped until I found my gun, and went to join the cop in pursuit of Fayard.

I came up on Swan from his left. He almost fired at me, but must have caught sight of my eye patch, because he made an expression of disgust and turned away. I drew next to him and whispered, "Troca's gone."

"You let him get away?"

"He's swimming with the fishes." I checked my gun to be sure it would fire. "I have one round left."

"So do I."

"Where's Fayard."

"Fayard? Is that this asshole's name?"

"What do you care? Where is he?"

"Over by the ditch-digger. But he's been quiet for a while, so he may have moved out."

"Okay. I'll go left and you go—"

"Right," he ordered. "Now."

It was my turn to express disgust.

We split up and circled the earthmover, coming back together on the other side.

"Terrific," I breathed. "He could be anywhere now."

The monorail whizzed above our heads and George raised his voice so I could hear him. "There's got to be a phone at the construction entrance. Let's circle around and I'll call for backup."

"Besides" I said, "the explosives are back there and we don't want him to get anywhere near them. He's nuts."

We both kept low and worked our way back to the where the dairy truck full of explosives sat, as if it had just finished its delivery route. George went searching for a phone, while I waited by the truck, standing guard with my last bullet. I sniffed the air and discovered that the evening's exertion had cleared my sinuses. Good to know.

Except for the strip of motels across Harbor Boulevard, there were few other businesses in the area and the park was pretty secluded. I doubted that anyone had heard the shots in the dead of night, so getting any outside help probably depended on Swan and his phone call. I knew that I needed to keep a sharp watch, so I pulled the patch from my head and peered into night with both eyes.

It was very dark in many places and very still everywhere. I blinked and felt that sudden urge to spin around to confront impending doom. There was no one behind me.

My blurred vision began to clear more, almost back to normal. Maybe I didn't need the eye patch any more. Maybe I was going to be able to….

Something moved quickly in the distance by the gate. I moved with it.

As I came around the entranceway, I caught sight of Fayard running full tilt away from the park and back to the motels. He was too far away for me to risk my single bullet. I took off after him, yelling back to wherever George was, "He's heading back to the cars at the motor court!"

I cut across the deserted four-lane boulevard after my man. I had to assume that he was still armed, so I ducked and weaved like a halfback among the shrubs and vehicles, trying to keep him in sight.

I lost him once briefly and then spotted him again bent low beside a DeSoto sedan, three cars over from where I'd parked my Kaiser. I glanced around to see if Swan was coming for an assist. When I looked back, Fayard had the DeSoto's starter whining. I wiped a palm across my eyes to clear my vision and felt an electric buzz of pain. *Damn.*

I tried to aim through it all as the car began to move. I fired my last shot and starred the windshield, missing my quarry. The DeSoto sped up, squealing tires out of the parking lot.

There was nothing else I could do, except run to my crate and give chase north up the boulevard.

When I got to the highway, Fayard fooled me, hanging a U-turn across the four lanes, and flew past me on the other side of the road, now heading south. I spun the Kaiser around and was almost doing sixty-five by the time I reached Katella Avenue and followed him west as we flashed along beside the railroad tracks. I got lucky and caught the green. But at Brookhurst Street, I had to run a red light. I almost hit a produce truck and swung the wheel frantically, fishtailing wildly, barely missing the rear end before flooring it again and continuing on. The engine wound tight, screaming.

We flashed past Route 39, Beach Boulevard. I tried to figure how I was going to stop him and decided that I wasn't. I could only hope to hang with him until some new factor came into play. Then, he pulled another Uee on me and headed back east to Beach.

I slammed on the foot brake, pulled the hand brake to lock the tires, and threw the Kaiser into a heart-stopping 180-degree bootlegger's skid. All four tortured tires screamed as I completed the maneuver, burning rubber, but finally getting the vehicle turned around, speeding through my own tire smoke. I took a thirty-mile-an-hour left behind him on Route 39 and almost flipped the car as the right-side tires slammed hard against the far curb. But I stayed upright as I hit the gas and headed north again behind him.

The Kaiser was taking a licking like a Timex, as we zoomed past Knott's Berry Farm on the left. I was done fooling around with this guy. He'd shot Suzi, wounded me, and been party to my abduction, twice. *Walk with grace, my ass.* I seriously started thinking about ramming him, if I could just catch up.

We both raced across South Avenue on the red and would have rocketed on into Orange County together, but when we could pass under the Santa Ana Freeway, he peeled left and made it over the Southern Pacific rail tracks as the crossing arm dropped down. I screeched to a shuddering halt in order not to hit the red and white guard arm, not to mention the silver Burlington Northern & Santa Fe train that barreled across my path.

Through the flickering gaps between the passing rail

cars, I watched the DeSoto's tail lights shrivel and finally fade to black.

CHAPTER 21

The inside of the Parker Center, south of City Hall, was pure cop shop. Even at this late hour, the lobby was busy with uniforms and suits herding wide-eyed citizens into an eight-floor maze.

Here, George assumed his full persona of Lieutenant of Detectives Swan, as he flashed his shield and had me buzzed through a door. We walked together with a platoon of other cops down a scuffed, painted third-floor hallway, past pictures of the command structure and a bulletproof glass divider, separating the public areas from the police desks in back. Somewhere a teletype chattered fitfully and phones rang, even though it was the middle of the night.

I'd been here before and I knew I'd be back again

someday, given my line of business. I kept my mind relaxed but attentive. Most of the cops seemed to be operating at the level of plumbers, but they were smart enough to take my gun. There was one official with a desk here who knew me from past cases and I thought I could trust, but unfortunately, Captain Seidman happened to be out of town on vacation at Lake Arrowhead. I was on my own in the wilds of copland and the natives looked restless.

Lieutenant Swan sat me alone in an office and started giving me *his* line of business, but he couldn't help adding a few personal questions about my relationship with Suzi. The guy really seemed to care about her.

"I've known her since we were kids," I told him. "And what's that got to do with what we went through tonight?"

"Did you ever…you know?"

I figured he deserved a punch, even if it was only verbal. "Yeah, once we were eating a string of licorice and I ate past my half."

His eyes caught fire. I could see him slowly come back, remembering where we were. He reached into a desk drawer and took out a fresh pack of Raleigh's, tore away the wrappings, and stuffed the coupon in his pants pocket. *Probably how he earned his badge.*

The smoke made my nerves itch and I wanted a cigarette, bad. All the guys in the squad room seemed to have one. Why not me too? What was I trying to prove? If cigarettes were going to torture me, it was only fair that I torture one back. But my sinuses were clear now, so—I decided to hold off the urge for a little longer, even in these smoke-filled quarters.

An elderly patrolman came in, started asking still more questions, and made notes on a steno pad with a mechanical pencil. He was a tired-faced man, probably approaching retirement, with a confident manner and calm voice. He asked about my background and wanted to see my license, but couldn't have been nicer about it. Maybe I owed him money.

I gave the cops all I knew about Thomas Fayard and the apparent communist plot. I told them I'd had a run in with the goateed guy up at Lost Valley and they could check with the Palmdale police. I didn't mention Walt or the dead astronaut. Things were complex enough without revealing my client or his inquiry. They assured me that they'd get out an APB for Fayard and a DeSoto with a bullet-fractured front window.

Troca's body had been recovered from the submarine pool and identified. There didn't seem to be any love lost on him by the police. In fact, there was a mild air of celebration about the whole thing.

The truck with the explosives, I learned, had been gone over by the crime-lab, but it wasn't unusual for a construction company to have access to explosives. The quantity and location, however, was more than unusual. The cop with the steno pad mentioned army surplus. I suggested they look into Reliance Management on that point and began to grow tired of all the questions and bad coffee.

Swan supplemented my story from time to time, appearing to hold a grudge against deadly attacks from idiots like Troca and Fayard. Who could blame him?

A middle-aged desk sergeant joined our party. He had one of those deeply pockmarked complexions that looked like he'd had trouble learning to eat with a fork when he was a kid. He looked at me, cleared his throat, and leaned over to whisper something into the lieutenant's ear. Swan's eyebrows went up. He lifted the receiver of the phone on his desk, punching a button on its base. "Swan speaking…Yes, sir." He glared at me. "I understand, sir." He made a face at me, as if I was a used cat food bowl, and glanced at the sergeant. "Yes, sir. Right away."

Somehow, I knew that Walt had been informed of the assault on his park and had expressed his concern to either the chief of police, the mayor, or Broderick Crawford.

The pebbly-faced sergeant took the opportunity to ask me, "You Stan Wade?"

I nodded.

"Stan Wade, detective?"

"Uh, yeah." I had a pretty good idea what was coming next.

"What's with that? Some kind of alias?" the cop asked. "Like Sam Spade?

I sighed. "It's real, pal. Get used to it."

Swan dropped the phone receiver into its cradle and said mildly, "Lay off him, Joe." Then he addressed me like we were cousins. "Well, Mr. Wade, that about it?"

He hated this and I couldn't help smiling. "Yeah, pretty much." I stood up. "Will that be all, Lieutenant?"

It took him a few seconds before he could trust his voice. "Yes, I think so." He handed back my .38 S&W. "And don't leave town."

Sure, I thought, checking the chambers. I whistled the theme from "Dragnet" and walked out of there.

Outside Parker Center, over to the east, the sky grew slowly pink. From various directions and distances I started hearing church bells ringing out. The fulfilling, wholesome sound made me take a deep breath of morning air. I smiled. It was Easter Sunday and I was starving.

ᘓᘓᘓ

I drove on down to Redondo Beach and stopped at Bob's Big Boy for a stack of strawberry pancakes and several cups of decent coffee. Fatigue hung on me like a wet horse blanket and I probably smelled like one, as I read the *Hollywood Reporter* and *Sunday Times*. The newspaper headlines made the world outside of Hollywood seem like fiction. *Reds Hunt Dalia Lama By Air. Tibet communist rule difficult as long as he is free. US Considering Naval Blockade of Russia in Baltic and*

Black Sea Areas. Red Forces to Bolster Iraqi Army. And one story told me that the nation's military chiefs advised congress that the US would be invincible in an all-out war. Admiral Burke, chief of naval operations, said if Russia started an all-out war "we would break her back." My back wasn't feeling all that well either and the news turned my gut. Probably what they used to call "war jitters."

I paid my bill and, instead of cigarettes, bought a pack of Beeman's pepsin chewing gum from the girl at the counter. Maybe it would sooth my stomach. Instead, it made my mouth taste like tar. I spat the nasty stuff into a nearby trashcan and headed for my car.

I needed a way to find Fayard, and his sister was my best lead. At a payphone outside the restaurant, I called Juliette's number, but got no answer. I could drive over to Oceanside and try to catch her at her swanky apartment, but a wave of exhaustion had replaced my jitters and I knew I was not functioning at my best. Then, the engine of my faithful Kaiser started missing. It had taken a tough beating over the last few days and now needed tender care. Come to think of it, so did I.

I found a Phillips 66 station a couple of blocks from where the *Cervantes II* was docked and listened while the young, pimply guy there told me the timing sounded off. Since it was a quiet Sunday, he didn't have much going on and thought he could do a tune-up and minor repairs, plus gas, oil, water, and air for the balding tires, all for a reasonable price. That was fine with me. I left the car in his greasy hands and walked to the cabin cruiser. I went below deck and placed the Sunday comics section in the stack I'd saved over the last few years. It was a ritual I'd performed on and off since I was a kid.

I knew that Walt's commissioned strips were in there. Mickey, Donald, and the new one: Scamp. Someday I'd sit down and read them all, but not right now. Right now, I dropped my weary carcass onto my bunk and slept the sleep of the deep.

Cops with white paint on their faces and red balls on their noses wandered around clueless. Suzi and Juliette waved bye-bye at me from the cockpit of an X-15. I waved back, but the jets blurred into a black submarine. Troca and Captain Taffe floated face down together in the surf next to it. Fayard drove by in the DeSoto and yelled, "Bombs and gas and more bombs," while pointing a funny cigarette at my face.

I wanted a smoke, but not his brand and not from him. I asked Jack Benny what I should do, but he said he was thinking it over.

One of the rides at POP summersaulted me into the ocean in a perfect swan dive and I came to the surface to find Lex shaking my shoulder and insistently calling, "Hey, squirrel. Wake up."

Through my stupor, she informed me that she'd received notice from the dock master that the boat was moored illegally and had to be moved. She waved a sheet of paper at me. "I know it's bad news, but we've gotta take the old girl out again."

I yawned at her. "I think the situation has improved with the Mob. The thugs who were after me have been taken care of, or at least taken to task. We can likely take her home again, back to Del Ray Lagoon."

"If you say so."

After some discussion, Lex decided that she could chart a course back to our original slip. I promised to pay her for her time and she said that thirty bucks would cover it, which reminded me that I was getting low on walking around money. While Lex warmed up the engines, I dug into the coffee can under the aft lockers and transferred four twenties from my stash to my wallet, leaving the can empty. I washed up, went "poof" with Stopette under my arms, put on my last clean dress shirt. Walking down the gangplank, I waved to Lex and headed back to the filling station, hoping that the young mechanical doctor had healed my car.

౧౯౬౯౩

It was mid-afternoon, with a bright sky full of puffy clouds—the sort of day we seldom got in LA. There was little point in returning to the warehouse where the AWA had held their meeting. No one of any importance would still be there and the police would have it under surveillance. So I pulled onto the PCH, heading for Manhattan

Beach and Juliette's apartment. The day's refreshing sea breeze continued coming in from the vast Pacific. I could almost smell pineapples, as I rang the buzzer and found her dressed to the nine's with coiffed hair and full makeup. Her outfit was a sleek and sophisticated formfitting black skirt with a black ruffled cardigan over a black knit top.

"Going to dinner this early?" I asked as she stepped past me and locked the door to her apartment. "You look lovely."

"Ah, Mr. Wade." She smiled with a cute tilt of her head. "I have additional scenes to shoot at Universal. This is my costume as an ingénue." She spun around for me to get the full impression. The fluted skirt twirled just enough to show a shapely calf. "You like?"

"Very much. It brings out your eyes."

She laughed musically. "Yours, as well."

I felt my face warming. "Please allow me to drive you, and perhaps we can share dinner again after you've finished."

"*D'accord,*" she agreed emphatically.

For the first time in a long time, I actually enjoyed driving in frantic LA traffic. She pretended not to notice the Kaiser's damaged window while leaning forward to find a classical music station on the car radio. I took the opportunity to slip in a question about her brother.

"I'm sorry, but I have not seen or heard from him for several days," she said as we sped northwest through the

Cahuenga Pass on the Hollywood Freeway. "It sometimes happens that way. He has his own life, too, you understand. Is it important?"

"Honestly," I said, still pretending to be an exec from Walt's company, "it could be a problem. The studio has learned that you both are in the country on temporary visas and that he has past ties to some dangerous political parties back in Europe. There's even a strong suspicion that he might be working undercover for the Soviets."

She bought my bluff and began to protest, defending her brother's honor. I told her that the evidence was fairly convincing and mentioned that he'd even been seen attending last night's meeting of the American Worker's Alliance. Her reaction was a combination of fear and stunned surprise. "I cannot believe it. He has strong opinions, but—"

"But it would explain why you haven't seen him lately. Are you absolutely sure that you are safe?"

She trapped her lip in thought and studied me a little longer, comparing what she knew to what I'd told her, evaluating it all. She grew quiet and seemed to begin to accept it by the time we arrived at the gate to the back lot. I told the guard that I was delivering Juliette DeLibre here for retakes in an episode of the *Steve Canyon* program. He nodded sagely, checked his clipboard, and let us enter the 300-plus acre "dream factory." I knew that the lot had been bought by the Music Corporation of America a few months earlier and renamed Revue Studios, but the signs still said what they had for over thirty years: Universal.

We parked near Sound Stage Eight, where she was greeted by an assistant director. I hung back while she went through her scenes with Dean Fredericks in uniform as the comic-strip air force man. He was dressed almost exactly like Major Scott up at the Edwards air force base.

For the next two hours, Juliette performed with elegance and grace, as the director made her repeat her lines before each take with the camera. Seeing her there, playing a role, I wondered about her relationship with her brother. I hoped he wasn't taking advantage or manipulating her. I knew that he'd gone to ground somewhere and hoped he wasn't hiding back at her apartment. I needed an excuse to search her digs, but couldn't think of a good one there in the movie studio, surrounded by all the props from past productions. A few feet from where I was standing, I saw something left over from *Touch of Evil.* A sign read, *Have You Forgotten Anything?* I had to laugh. It was things like that that distracted me from more pressing matters.

Another was the painting of Karloff as the Mummy, off to my right. A grip walked by, noticed that I was staring at it, and whispered: "Can you believe it? Some company in England is making its own mummy movie now. It ain't like the good old days."

He shook his head and moved on like the ghost of Hamlet's father. I shrugged, recalling an earlier case that

I'd worked back in August of 1956. Karloff had appeared on the *Ernie Kovacs Show*, right around the time that Bela Lugosi had died of a heart attack. At least, that's what the gentle British actor and I had reported to the police.

Juliette finished her scenes and came back to me, holding out both hands, like Loretta Young.

"Now, how about that dinner?" I smiled.

"I am famished," she said. "Where shall we go?"

Dusk had fallen as I drove out Sunset between Gower and Vine, taking a chance that we could get seated at the Moulin Rouge supper club. We held hands during the short trip and listened to *Johnny Dollar* on the radio as he solved a murder at Lake Mead in less than 30 minutes.

A billboard in the lobby of the dinner theatre announced that the Eleventh Annual Emmy's would take place here at the theater in early May. Luck was with me and I got us a nice table near the front of the stage for only a twenty-dollar tip to the maître d'. The food was excellent and the conversation stayed light. I could see that Juliette noticed I wasn't smoking. She seemed happy about it and so was I.

After our dinner of scallops—she called them Coquilles St, Jacques—we enjoyed drinks and watched the opening act, a twangy guitar duo called the Ventures, followed by Frankie Laine and Johnny Ray performing together in a "Frankie and Johnny Review." Johnny wore his hearing aid and Frankie wore his black-framed glasses. Johnny sang and cried about his sweetheart. Frankie sang about being forsaken by his darling. All the crying and forsaking didn't dampen *our* spirits though, or keep us from sitting close and catching each other's eye.

On the drive back through the velvety night to her apartment, we became even closer, as she leaned her head on my shoulder.

At the door, I accepted the keys from her slim hand and unlocked the latch. "There's something else I need to tell you."

She gave me a coy smile. "Is this your clever way to get into my quarters?"

I couldn't help chuckling. We moved inside together as if we'd been dating for months, and she immediately set about fixing us a nightcap and putting on some music on the console stereo. Sinatra sang "You're Sensational" with full orchestral accompaniment.

I took the opportunity to subtly scan the room, trying to see any indication that her brother was possibly there. Rich, mahogany furniture on a white pile carpet. Modern art on the paneled walls. No unusual cigarette butts in the ashtrays. No odd sounds from the other rooms. No indents in the cushions of the low couch or plush chairs. I relaxed a little in the room's indirect lighting.

She was mixing vodka martinis when I came over to the mini-bar and asked, "Do you have anything that tastes of scotch?"

There was no disappointment in her hazel eyes. She

smiled and raised an elegant palm, gesturing to a green bottle behind the bar. I poured my own drink over ice and we clinked glasses, moving to the sofa.

"*A la votre*," she toasted.

"Happy days." We drank and I turned the conversation to a topic I'd covered earlier. "Captain Taffe, I understand, was preparing to give to you his air force ring."

She blinked very long lashes. "Yes?"

"Were you aware that he was intending to ask for your hand in engagement?"

She sipped her drink and spoke frankly. "Yes, but I was not sure it should be. It is an important decision. I asked him for a little time to consider."

She was quiet.

"And…"

She set her glass next to mine on the end table. "And…I reluctantly concluded that I did not love him. He was in the end, as you say, not my type."

The record changer moved its arm and we were lifted into the vibrato world of Edith Piaf. I self-consciously scratched an itch on the left side of my face and felt a sting from my stitches.

"Oh, your wound is still painful. Let me help you." She rose and went to the bedroom, leaving the door ajar. I could see part way into the room, while she rummaged in a dresser drawer.

"Be still," she said, coming back to me with a small pair of scissors.

I felt a gentle tugging and twinge at the side of my face, as she bent and snipped at my sutures.

Stepping back, she turned her head to one side to inspect her work. "There," she said, satisfied.

This time, her eyes seemed to draw me all the way into her. She breathed, "You are my type." She pulled me gently back to the sofa.

We moved closer. She flipped her hair and I smelled of soap and shampoo. I ran my hand under her hair, massaging the warm skin at the back of her neck. She quivered and closed her eyes, and I tasted the deliciousness under her ear.

She tilted her chin up and parted her lips. I grazed her cheek and kissed her on the mouth.

She kissed me tentatively at first, then deeply. Her tongue slipped into my mouth and her body pressed hard against me. I felt the sudden driving heat of shared passion. We fumbled with zippers and buttons, pulling off our clothes in a desperate attempt to find each other. She was quickly down to her bra and panties and unbuckling my belt, helping me shed the rest of my clothes.

Her fingers felt cool encircling me, and it was all I could do to restrain myself.

She held me lightly and guided me into her. Her breath quickened, dictating the pace of our lovemaking. She escalated us higher and higher, going into orbit before we both climaxed. We inhaled each other, holding tight, lying like that, out of breath for several minutes.

Then she said, "Someday, you must tell me of the white streak in your hair. It's *tres* sexy."

CHAPTER 22

The long golden fingers of dawn reached through the window and gently stroked my eyes open. Juliette and I lay like two question marks in her bed, having moved there during the night. Her back was against my front, her skin warming my thighs and her hair tickling my nose. I inhaled the scent of her shampoo and listened to her low, even breathing.

With slight regret, I eased my body away from hers and slipped out from under the sheets. She stirred and fell back to peaceful slumber, as I dressed. I could find no signs of her brother in the apartment. I did, however, find some medicated cream and a Band-Aid which I applied to my unstitched brow. I took a final gaze at her sleeping body, wrote her a note, and quietly exited the apartment.

Why was I leaving? Why not stay and enjoy the day with sweet Juliette DeLibre? It wasn't easy to stray from the warmth of her touch. But I reminded myself that I was on an assignment and I'd been lucky so far. And I still wasn't ready to butt out.

⌘

I stood in the cool, calm shadows outside her building wanting a cigarette and reviewing my situation. Okay, my idea of getting a lead on Fayard through his sister hadn't worked out. She had no idea where he might be. That was both good and bad. Either way, it left me high and dry. We'd slept in together and it was now mid-morning. My head was a little groggy and stuffy, so I climbed into the Kaiser and went searching for coffee.

I had slept later than I'd planned and still felt romantic enough to enjoy the car radio that played "Since I Don't Have You" and "The Happy Organ." I switched it off when it started into some silly song about Charlie Brown, he's a clown, and drove on over to my office at the Brown Derby.

As I pulled into the lot behind the restaurant, I gave the car phone a test and got hold of Norman. He was busy at work in the back of the TV and electronics shop, but I managed to let him know that he'd been right about Fayard being a communist and for him to let *me* know if and when the sleazebag ever came into the store again.

Before I unlocked my office, I saw Cindy hard at work at her adding machine, so I collected two mugs of black coffee and wandered over to offer her one. She had on the blue dress with the white trim that I liked. Her desk was as cluttered as a spice rack. She perked up when she saw me and put a file folder down on the floor next to her cushioned swivel chair. "Where have you been, Stan?"

"Here and there." I shrugged and smiled. "Now and then, this place and that, and how are you Mrs. Pyle?"

"What happened to your eye?"

"I ran into an old friend a few days ago, literally."

"I told you your job was dangerous." Since I'd forgotten cream and sugar, she set her coffee aside on top of a green and tan ledger book. "Well, it looks better now."

"Feels better, too. Thanks. How's Jimmy?"

"He's all excited now about rockets and outer space. He wants to grow up to be just like Buzz Cory, whoever that is."

"I think he's a commander of the *Space Patrol* on TV."

"Is that someone you know?"

"No, but I bet Norman does. Maybe personally."

She twirled a silvery bang at the side of her head and considered. "He's weird."

I sipped my coffee and scalded the tip of my tongue. "Sometimes," I agreed. "Not always. What's cooking here? And I don't mean in the kitchen."

"Mr. Cobb has a pile of accounts that he wants you to follow-up on. I slid them under your door. Oh, and a customer tried to steal the caricatures of Jimmy Cagney and Adolph Hitler."

"Hitler?"

"Oops. I mean Menjou. Carlos caught him, so I guess that's taken care of."

"Crime marches on, eh?"

"I guess." Her blue eyes drifted down to her desk and I could tell that she'd started thinking about her work again.

"Well, tell Jimmy that I just might know a few *real* space guys and maybe I can get him an autographed picture of one."

She thought that would be "grand," which was one of the things I liked best about Cindy. She sometimes seemed to have stepped right out of a '30s double feature.

I walked over and unlocked my office door, closing it behind me. The place was still a mess, so I spent time sorting the mail and filling the wastebasket. Finally, I got another cup of coffee and sat down to dial long distance. I was at a dead end, trying to locate Fayard and I need inspiration. I gave the operator Mr. P's number and she said to hold the line until the circuits to Hawaii cleared. I filled the time fetching a few extra twenties from my cash box and looking over the accounts that Cindy had slipped under my door.

I calculated that, since Honolulu was three hours behind the west coast, it would be about 9 a.m. there. He'd be up by then, for sure.

After the operator got the connection, I heard his familiar, gravelly voice in my ear. "Hello, Stan. How are things in the city of angels?"

"More like the city of angles, sir. I'm calling 'cause I need your help."

"Sure, kid. But first tell me how Gunther is doing."

I thought I could hear the surf in the background, but it was probably just a bad connection. "He seems to be doing well, sir. I went to see him the other day and he said to send his regards. How's the wife?"

"Carman is fine, kid. We both are a couple of happy retirees in paradise. I just can't seem to get a decent taco anywhere on the big island."

"I'll see if I can send you one air mail."

He chuckled and told me he was working as a story consultant on a new PI show there for Warner Brothers. "They keep having me wire the mainland with bits of local color and plot points for their scenes at a sound stage near you." I could almost hear him shake his head when he said, "Leave it to crazy Hollywood to film a Hawaiian show in Los Angles."

I commiserated for a moment and then filled him in on my latest case, letting him know that I was stuck and needing advice.

"Hmmm…Based on what you've just told me, I can think of a couple things you should try."

A fly buzzed around my tiny office and landed upside down on the ceiling. "All right." I stretched the phone cord over to the door and opened it so the fly could do an Emmelman and leave. "I'm listening."

"First, it sounds like you need to confront Walt. Back him into a corner or trick him into telling you at least part of the truth. I remember that there were rumors about his involvement with the FBI, but that was years ago. He could be in a lot deeper now and know a lot more than he's telling you."

"You're right, of course. He seems to have a fair amount of pull with the military operations at the air base and there are bodyguards keeping him under close surveillance. He's worried about something big."

"Then get him to tell you. Remind him about how I stopped those spies from reaching him when he was making that *Victory Thru Air Power* cartoon during the war. He owes me and you can make use of the debt."

"Okay. You said there were a couple of things I could try. What was the other?"

Somehow the fly had gotten back in. It hovered and landed on a pile of pulp mystery magazines stacked on top of my lone file cabinet.

"Detective work 101, kiddo. Unless there's big money involved, '*cherche la femme.*'"

I held the phone receiver at arm's length and stared at it. The fly sounded like it was laughing at me. "Uh, you're right, sir. I forgot to mention that Fayard and his sister are here from France."

"You see?" he said. "101. Get close to her and I'll bet you'll find him."

I almost blushed. "I'll be sure to get right on that, again." I bit down on my lip to keep from snickering.

"Don't try too hard to be a hero," he said from across the waves. "I know you and you'll want to leap a tall building, or something. Just work the case with honor and careful determination, Stan. And call me back after you've solved it."

"Will do, sir. Good to talk to you. Enjoy your retirement. You've earned it."

I heard his smile. "My back tells me that very thing every morning, Stan. Good talking to you, too."

We hung up before I thought to tell him what I had almost done the other day with his gun. Maybe that was for the best. I sat there a while, doing nothing, and when I looked up, the fly had flown.

❧❧❧

My next stop was back at the lagoon to see if Lex had docked the *Cervantes II*. I needed a shave and change of linen.

The boat sat high in the water and bobbed a little from a strong westerly breeze. The clouds above had thickened and grayed. I went aboard and cleaned up.

There was a note from Lex saying that she planned to catch a bus back to her place and I should throw out the loaf of bread in the food locker because it had turned green.

While whittling at my face with the safety razor, I saw now that I had a slight scar over my left eye to go with the streak in my hair. If my career kept up in this manner, in a few years, they'd say I looked like Boris Karloff. But my vision was clear, so I assumed there was no serious damage to my cornea, or retina, or other eyeball parts.

I rummaged through my laundry bag and found that the only thing wearable was a red Hawaiian shirt covered with yellow surfboards. In honor of Mr. P. I shrugged it on and went to see my favorite Jap.

ೕೂೕ

Just about everyone I knew between the ages of twenty-five and sixty-five had a local bar or tavern that they frequented for drink, food, and a bit of companionship. For me, it was a bonus if the place had a phone I could use to make calls or get messages. The Blue Phrog was a beached tugboat near the inlet of the lagoon, where the beer was fresh, the ham-and-cheese sandwiches were fresh and the waitresses were…well, Sunny seldom had any waitresses.

The beached boat sat at an angle off its keel and

Shunryu "Sunny" Goh, its sole owner and barkeep, had all the tables and benches built at a compensating slant, so your drinks wouldn't slide off or roll overboard. Sunny himself was a little lopsided, having lost his left arm to the elbow in a fight with Komodo dragon, or so he claimed. I'd heard that the truth was he'd caught his shirtsleeve in a conveyor assembly at a Rockwell plant years ago, but neither he nor I ever gave away each other's secrets. You'd think we were magicians. Maybe we were.

Sunny was wrestling with the rabbit ears of the small TV that sat high on a shelf full of bottles behind the bar, when I dropped in. He tried and failed to get the local news, then a Dodgers game, finally settling on an episode of *The Millionaire*.

"Better than those damn soap operas," he grumbled. Then he said what everybody did when they watched the show: "Wish someone would give *me* a check for a million dollars." He slung a limp towel over his shoulder and came over to get my order or give me grief. Probably both. "Seen Lex lately? Her tab's getting up there."

On weekend evenings, Sunny hired folksingers to sing and strum on a stage he had built out on the tug's stern. I let my gaze drift that way to a sky full of clouds. "I'll cover her tab. How much is it?"

He cracked open a bottle of Black Label and set it on the bar's worn surface in front of me. "Never mind."

Foam dribbled down the dark neck of the chilled bottle. I took a swig and half-heartedly shook beer from my hand. "No, I'll pay it. I owe her. How much?"

He scratched the back of an ear. "Call it fifty bucks."

Beer went down my windpipe. I coughed and reached for my wallet. "Seriously?"

He shrugged. "What can I say? It's been building up."

I gave him three twenties and he gave me back a ten, gesturing at my bottle. "That one's on the boat." He got out a pack of Chesterfields and offered me one.

I thought about it, hard. "No, thanks. Hand me the phone, will you? I need to make a couple of local calls."

He slung the phone and its cord from next to the cash register and placed it on the bar beside my hand that was peeling at the bottle's label.

I caught the Bakelite receiver between my chin and shoulder and spun the dial. Two minutes later, I was complaining, "Come on, Walt. I need answers. You can trust me. Fill me in, or I'll walk."

"Stan, you should know by now that I can't talk about details over the phone."

"Then I'll come to you," I pressed. "But we've got to talk."

"No, I'm tied up in meetings all day. That's why I need you to keep following up on this for me." The TV was running a stupid Brylcreem commercial. "All I can tell you is that what you're doing is important, perhaps even vital, to our nation's security."

"I don't need a pep talk. I need facts." Gunther had said I should walk with grace, but it didn't feel like grace wanted to walk with me. "You owe me. Now, give me something I can use, dammit."

Sunny gave me a sharp oriental glare from down the end of the bar and I turned to face the other direction.

"Let's say, Fayard's name has been linked to several other passings of military men in Europe, understand?" Walt said. "And there appears to be another player higher up behind the curtain giving instructions." The commercial switched to Ipana toothpaste. Brusha-brusha. "Look, while I greatly appreciate how you've protected the park and will compensate you appropriately, I can only tell you that there's also an unseen war going on that is neither cold, nor what you read about in the newspapers."

"What are you saying?"

"Just that our military and industrial organizations need strengthening, as well as oversight and review. The public wants a powerful defense against the Reds, but the danger is that it can become too powerful."

I didn't like the way that sounded, especially coming from Walt. Either, he was starting to slip from the strain, or we were all in for more trouble than we knew. I resisted the urge to rest my head on the cool surface of the bar. The attack on his park must have really un-nerved him. I decided to try and talk him down. "Listen, you know you can depend on me, right? I just want to get to the truth, like a good little detective."

"I know, Stan. We all want the truth. And you'll get it—eventually."

Great. Maybe if I came at him from another direction. "Then at least tell me this: do you know anything about a white-haired man who seems to have a lot of pull with the American Worker's Alliance?"

Walt's voice became even more firm than before. "Stay away from them, Stan. Other people are working that side of the street. Just concentrate on what happened to our pilot, like I asked you. I've spoken to Colonel Scott and his PR man at the base and I agree with them that this needs to be finalized and kept quiet. We can't have any hint of stain on Project Mercury. It's important that the country has someone to look up to during this race for space."

The TV was telling me to be sociable, look smart, and drink light, refreshing Pepsi. I took a deep breath. "Who writes your dialogue, Davy Crockett?"

I think I hear him sigh. Then: "Davy was independent and succeeded in getting things done. He fought for what he thought was right. A true American legend. That's the sort of inspiration we all need today and the project will give it to us."

I understood what he was driving at and knew I wasn't getting the full story, just the general outline. I still didn't like it, but I said, "Okay, Walt, okay. But when this is all over, 'Lucy, you gotta lot a 'splaining to do.'"

❧❧❧

I signaled to Sunny for another Black Label and he ambled over with it. "You done tying up my phone line? I might get an important call."

"Who from?" I crabbed. "The Board of Health? Gimme a ham and cheese sandwich, will you?"

He grunted and moved away to serve a little, balding guy who had just eased down at the other end of the bar, wearing red suspenders as bright as my shirt. He might have been Elisha Cook, but my mind was elsewhere.

The news came on the TV and I watched indifferently as various reports of car crashes, Easter egg hunts, and memorial services for Lou Costello filled the tiny screen. I recalled a different funeral that I'd missed due to all of this. Gregory Peck was interviewed about our nation's stockpile of tabun nerve gas. He said it posed a threat, because a storage tank hit hard enough could drift a deadly cloud across a populated area. Sounded like a normal day in LA to me.

Sunny came back with my sandwich order, along with a bag of chips. "This all's going on your tab now, you know." Despite his missing arm, I'd heard that he held a black belt in karate or something and should therefore not be messed with. I quietly burped my thanks.

Outside, the wind had picked up and the clouds continued rolling in from the west. Inside, I ate and drank and thunk. I finished the meal and said to the barkeep,

"One last phone call, promise," and dialed Granger-74000. Juliette's apartment.

It rang three times. The guy with the suspenders took a long, loving pull on a cigarette. The TV told me Pall Malls were outstanding and mild. Juliette told me that she'd heard from her brother and knew where to find him.

CHAPTER 23

The overcast continued to thicken as we drove through the San Gabriel Mountains and neared the town of Acton. A cool, wet wind blew in from the mountains and I thought about stopping to get a full glass of beer, but shrugged it off.

The nickel-plated sky made the drive seem longer this time, but the company was good. At first, I'd been against taking Juliette along, but she'd begged from the heart, a small tear sliding down her freckled cheek, when telling me of her brief encounter with her brother. She was like a nun desperate to save a drowning child.

"It was not possible for me to stop him," she'd said when I'd met her at her apartment. "He was a man possessed by fear and determination."

Fayard had tried to take her with him, but she'd held back, not telling him that she intended to contact me. He was going back to the farm in the Lost Valley in a truck he'd boosted from somewhere and he planned what Juliette called the *sacrifice ultimate*. I was pretty sure I knew what that meant and I'd been to the farm once before, so I knew how to find him.

Juliette wanted to appeal to him one last time, sister to brother. Regardless of how he'd treated her in the past, she still wanted to urge him to redemption. She hadn't noted the plate number of his truck, of course, recalling only that it was light blue with a brown tarp stretched across the bed. We hadn't spotted it yet during our drive to the ranch. I just hoped that the rain would hold off, so I wouldn't have to navigate through the hills on bad roads during a storm.

Even though we were in the mountains, I gave the car phone a try and was amazed that this time I could contact Norman. It must have had something to do with the gathering atmospheric conditions. I kept our conversation brief and as logical as Norm would allow, telling him to alert the police and inform them of the farm's general location.

Juliette watched me steer the Kaiser and talk on the phone. She listened while I told her about Norman and his exotic perspectives and inventions.

"Your friend sounds *tres outré*, yes?"

"And a little *macabre*, too," I agreed, showing off

my one year of college French. I was proud of myself for having remembered that much. "But I think we can depend on him to follow through. Just hope the police can contact the Highway Patrol and get us some backup locating your brother."

"He was terribly nervous," she said, as we stopped to fill the Kaiser's tank at an Eagle station off Elizabeth Lake Road. "I must make him listen; make him understand that we mean him no harm."

I didn't answer. Instead, I bought us a couple of Pepsis from the squat, red vending machine in front of the station and paid the attendant for the gas, plus deposit on the pop bottles.

He liked my red shirt and said "Aloha" as I put the car into gear and moved it again down the road.

Juliette had grown quiet, staring ahead with eyes that seemed to burn with brave intensity. "I'm sorry," she said in a quiet voice. "He gave me no choice."

I kept my voice calm. "What do you mean?"

"We must go back." Her accent was clouded with emotion. "He made me lead you here."

"I was hoping that wasn't the case, Juliette."

She seemed surprised, but quickly understood. "So—so we go back now, yes?"

"This may be the best chance at getting him, but it's your choice. We go on, if you agree."

"You're cruel," she said. "You're making me choose."

I slowed the car. "Do you want me to choose for you?"

"I don't know," she said, touching fingers lightly to my sleeve.

I recalled a scene in Casablanca where Ingrid begged Bogie to decide for both of them. "Then we go on?" I urged.

She took a shuddering breath and nodded her head resignedly. "He is my only brother…"

"I know."

"We *must* help him."

I grunted, following a turn in the highway. "Or stop him." A frayed asphalt ribbon of road climbed into the surrounding slopes of the foothills and curved slightly around big bare stones, past a stand of black oaks and a growth of jack pines. A dirt road went higher up. We twisted through a heavily wooded canyon dark enough to be in the middle of a redwood forest and swerved sharply around several big trees. When we reached the cutoff that led to Lost Valley Ranch Road, I dimmed my lights in order not to alert anyone of our arrival and soon parked in the same spot away from the farm that Suzi had used earlier in the week. I decided to give Juliette my gun for protection. I passed it to her. "Do you have any idea how to use this?"

She looked demure and half smiled. "I performed in an episode of *Gunsmoke* once and had to shoot an Indian—in the back." She shivered slightly.

I smiled and said, "Ugh," to lighten the mood. "Well, honey, I guess that'll have to do, but be careful, hear?" I took a switchblade from the glove compartment. I could use the knife with some slight skill, if necessary. Enough to be a threat. That and one other small trick was all I had left.

We got out onto the road and each quietly shut our car door. A cool breeze blew through the nearby gorge, past a huge fallen tree with a ten-foot, up-turned clot of earth trapped in its roots. A bird that I couldn't locate called mournfully. At least, I hoped it was a bird.

In the fading light, I could soon see the farmhouse clearly for the first time. The place was set back in a fold of the hills, with a big oak tree practically on the front porch. The barn at the side was shut up, but a light-colored Ford pick-up was parked beside it. I bent to feel the exhaust pipe. Still warm.

A bird called from high in the tree, but there was no answer. A dim light filtered from under a shade in a side window.

We walked along together like two cats, hunched in the shadows, approaching the window frame. Through the smudged glass, I saw a reclining form under the covers of a sagging bed.

I signaled her around to the front of the house and saw that the main entrance was open, except for the screen door. I tugged slightly at it and found it unhooked. Good news. I recalled that it squeaked. Bad news.

Juliette appealed to me in a low voice. "He will listen to me. Let me go and wake him."

I shook my head and answered quietly, "It's too dangerous. Stay behind me."

She lowered her eyes and nodded.

I needed to time our next move so Fayard wouldn't hear us. The radio was playing, but it was a soft murmur. Too low to trust that it would mask the sound from the screen door. The muted, approaching thunder might possibly be loud enough, but I had no way of predicting *how* loud or exactly when it would hit. In fact, if the rumble got any nearer, it might even wake him up. We couldn't wait.

Then I remembered the clock. I checked the glowing dial of my wristwatch and saw that it would be 11 p.m. in about three minutes. I waited what seemed like two weeks and checked it again, signaling to Juliette to stay back in the shadows. The second hand glided past the numeral six and started up to the twelve as I took a breath, let half of it out, and heard the cuckoo start calling inside the house.

The silly clock-sound covered the creak of the door when I dashed in and dove behind the low-slung couch. I tumbled once, sprang to my feet, clicked open the knife, and found the barrel of a .44 Magnum less than ten inches from my face, pointing directly at my undamaged eye.

"Son of a shit, man," Fayard said. "You're wigging me out."

Juliette called out to him over the sound of the squeaking door, "Thomas, do not shoot him, please."

I raised my hands and dropped the knife, hoping it would stick in his foot. No such luck.

Fayard's eyes danced with a slight twitch. He scratched at his bearded chin and looked over my shoulder. "What do you want me to do with him?"

I turned my head to see who he was addressing.

"I haven't decided yet," Juliette replied and broke open my revolver, shaking the cartridges into her palm.

I felt my heart accelerate, heard distant thunder, and saw her with fresh eyes.

She stood there smiling in a dark blue dress and matching blouse with an off-white Peter Pan collar. She got out a Gauloises cigarette from somewhere, lit it, came over, and blew smoke in my face.

It was hauntingly delightful.

Then she slapped me with a crack like a .22 and began a quick search of everything in my pockets.

I stood for it like the dope I was, feeling hurt in more ways than one. Finally, I said, "You can keep the pack of Beeman's gum. It's foul, like you."

She shook her head and made a *tut-tut-tut* sound, handing back my keys, wallet, and near-empty paper packet of pain pills.

Her brother laughed with mocking confidence. "Nice shirt man."

I knew I was trapped and didn't want to show it, but

couldn't stop myself from looking into Juliette's hazel eyes. "Damn. I didn't want it to go this way."

A faint frown touched the corners of her mouth. "*Tres heroic.*"

I remembered that Walt had told me that Fayard had been implicated in the deaths of several men overseas. Until now, I'd thought that he'd meant the goateed brother, not the actress sister.

The gun in Thomas Fayard's hand shook a little, as he asked Juliette, "The police? Are they coming here? They'll find the—"

"Shut!" Juliette hissed at him.

Fayard's tongue licked dry lips. It was a fair impersonation of a lizard. "It's ruined, he said. "The whole plan has gone south out of control."

"*You* are the one out of control," Juliette snapped. "A weak, addicted failure."

I broke in, challenging her. "And *you* were never in love with Taffe. You just wanted to get information from him."

Her odd smile came back. "And, my poor boy, I never really loved you as well. None of you Americans can be trusted. Did you know that your country secretly tested A-bombs in the upper atmosphere three times last year?"

"Your news organization doesn't tell you things like that, man," Fayard added from behind me. "It will all hang out eventually."

I turned my head to tell him, "You could be right, but it has nothing to do with me."

He had gained a genuine twitch in his left eyelid. "I don't believe that for a second, man. You know about the gas stored at the air force base. It's cats like you that'll cause thousands to die." His face glowed with perspiration and his eyes grew wide and whitened.

Now I *knew* I was surrounded by insanity.

Beyond the trees, lightning flashed like movie premiere. Juliette spoke in her strange yet lyrical voice. "Your president announced weeks ago that your country would launch a satellite every month later this year."

"I've had nothing to do with that."

Thunder from the lightning flash rumbled over our heads.

"You are all warriors in the cold, cold war," she said, smacking my empty gun repeatedly like a blackjack into her palm. But it was Fayard's .44 that worried me the most. I needed to get at it. Maybe I could cause him to stampede and then I could make a grab.

I turned to face him. "You thought you were pretty smart to come here, because you figured the cops would overlook a location they'd already searched. But the Highway Patrol told me they checked here every day, just in case you returned. They could be here any time."

He looked at me as if I were from another planet. "You hear that? We've got to split now!"

"Stop your panic, Thomas," she ordered. "I heard

him call them while on the way here, but it will be some time before they can arrive at this location."

"We've got to go. We've got to go!" He looked strung out and ready to crack.

Maybe I could help. "There's a car coming!" I shouted.

Fayard turned to the window and I grabbed for the gun.

Something hit me in the back of the head and my brain flew out into the cosmos and back. I fell to the floor, knowing that the blow had come from my own gun and a woman that I'd cared for.

My old buddy, the black-and-white clown paddled over next to me, prone on a surfboard. He wore a baseball umpire's outfit with a caged mask "He foiled our plan against the super-capitalist, Disney. It's time to execute plan B," someone said.

Fayard pulled nervously on his beard and started turning into a goat. "Baah, he knows too much."

Juliette floated down on an enormous cloud of smoke. "You have the explosives in the truck and know the way to the base."

I tried to slide into a position where I could hear better, but Jack Benny yelled, "Now cut that out!"

"Baaaad trip, baaaad trip. Even if the Party demands it," Fayard whined. The smoke and dark clouds rolled in, mingling with the smog. I heard snap and pop and crackle as I slid into home. The umpire clown bent and made a sweeping gesture with his hands, as if to signal that I was safe. But I knew that I was out.

CHAPTER 24

The world was upside down. My arms ached behind my back. Blood was rushing to my head. I couldn't find the ground beneath my feet. The light was bad and the wind was howling in the rafters.

I got my eyes into focus and realized I was *hanging* in the rafters, tied with a stout rope around my waist and wrists, at least fifteen feet above the dirt floor of the barn. I shook my head to clear out the smog and immediately regretted the act, mumbling, "Well, Stanley, here's another nice mess. I've never been hung out upside down before."

But it was a failed attempt at humor. The more my consciousness came back and the more reality pressed in, the more I knew my situation was desperate. The truth was that they had strung me up and no one was coming to help me get down. My gun and knife were gone. I'd been betrayed and held captive by a crazed commie and his two-faced, lying sister. I was lucky to still be alive—hanging here trussed up, ready to be shot at or just left to die from blood bursting my brain.

I tried taking deep breaths to calm myself. Then I tried to wiggle free. It only tightened the knots and spun me on the creaking rope. Someone shouted, "Sonofabitch!" at the top of their lungs and it was me.

My enemies must have heard me, because the next time I rotated around like a yo-yo dangling on a string, they stood at the barn door in the light of a lonely oil lantern.

Fayard was still protesting that they had to get away before the cops arrived. Juliette had the Magnum now and she raised it as if to strike him in the face. But she didn't complete the move, seeing her brother flinch and pull at his hair. She looked up at me. "We're leaving now, before the storm hits. Someday, maybe your friends will find you here." She tapped her small foot on the top the lantern that set on the straw-strewn floor. "Maybe the wind will blow over the lantern. Maybe—"

The pulse in my neck pounded and sparks flashed in my vision. "Maybe the sun will come up in the west, you Eastern-bloc bitch."

She startled me by laughing. "You are the most foolish man I have ever met."

"I'll be here all week," I answered. "Tip your wait-ress."

Fayard ignored all of this, clutching at his sister's arm. "I can't go without a fix. I need a fix. I need it bad."

I slowly rotated around on my rope and lost sight of them again, but I heard her say, "Come. I'll take care of you."

When I completed the turn, they were gone and I be-gan to pull at the Twist-O-Flex band on my left wrist.

In the vain cleverness of my youth, I'd taken a piece of razor blade and Scotch taped it to the back of my brother's watch, figuring that it would come in handy when my hands were tied behind my back. It seemed at first like a silly precaution, but I had escaped capture suc-cessfully a couple of times before with it, just not in such exotic conditions as these. Now my fingers felt like knackwursts and my nails couldn't get a good purchase to peel the blade free from under the tape on the watch's back. I doggedly picked at the edge of the tape and at last felt the blade lift slightly from the metal surface. I fum-bled it free and prayed to all the gods I'd ever heard of that I wouldn't drop it, as I started sawing at my ropes.

The rhythm of my back-and-forth cutting set me spinning again like a compass needle. Once, I sliced a finger and almost dropped the tiny blade. I could hear the first smacks of rain on the barn's tin roof as the rope started to give way. It wasn't until then that it fully oc-curred to me that I was about to fall fifteen feet down on my head. I stopped cutting, trying to think of a safer maneuver. Then two things happened. I heard gunfire from the farmhouse and the rope snapped.

☙❧

I came to within seconds, I think. I was on the floor barely breathing, my mouth full of barn dust and hay. My shoulder had popped out painfully. My knees ached like I'd been kicked a hundred times by Lou "The Toe" Groza.

The rain began falling with serious intent. I wobbled to a standing position and wiped sweat from my eyes. The left one stung me fully awake.

I heard the deep growl of a diesel engine starting up in the yard outside the barn. I slammed my dislocated shoulder against a rough-hewn barn pillar and yelped like a spanked pup as the bones crunched and popped back into place. Intense pain was my partner in crime. If I'd had access to it, I would have swallowed all the Darvon ever manufactured.

I hobbled on banged-up legs and then picked up the lantern. Slipping on the wet grass out in the yard, I flung the steaming thing at the passing truck. Juliette bounced in the driver's seat, laughing and steering away from the low splash of flames.

I staggered to the farmhouse, spitting out a least a pound of dirt. Fayard was on the floor in a pool of his own blood. I scanned the room for my gun, found it on a table, but still without bullets.

Fayard gurgled something behind me. I pressed a chair cushion to his chest where the bullets had gone in and the blood was coming out. His watery eyes wobbled. He smiled. "Stop her, man. The tabun gas—at the air base." He raised his head an inch and coughed blood. "Stop her. One freezing winter—she burned our mother to stay warm."

"What? No!"

His eyes dimmed and stilled their anxious movements. The rain outside crashed down so hard, I almost didn't catch his last words. "Far out, man. Too—too far."

❧❧❧

I scrambled through muck and rain, running for my car. I was soaking wet as I fired the engine and stomped the gas pedal.

She had at least a five-minute lead on me. I gritted my teeth and started after her.

The car swirled around as the rain hit my windshield in buckets. The wipers fought back the torrent. I squinted and tried to see the road ahead through my blurred headlights. I slid down a side road that slithered like a snake beneath my tires. Finally the road became paved again, but it didn't seem to tame my car as it continued to buck and skid.

The road was narrow and uneven, virtually one lane with ruts, especially at the turnouts. I couldn't do more than twenty-five.

The moving lights ahead told me I was only a couple of minutes behind her now.

I took the curves at a mad speed and the grades with zooming power.

The sound of the laboring engine was drowned out by the rain pelting the car roof. If the circumstances were less frantic, I might have enjoyed the sound.

I swung past a fallen branch the size of a rowboat and twice as wet, down into another wide canyon, gaining on her every second.

Suddenly, the road became a crooked tunnel bored through the black wall of night. Leafy trees flanked the twisty blacktop, their branches bent low with rainwater, interweaving overhead to shut out the sky. The road was empty ahead, its surface unwinding like dull-gloss film under the glare of the car's high beams. Twice I almost lost control on sharp curves, had to grind down on the brakes and power out of each skid.

The rain kept coming in torrents, pelting the Kaiser, its wipers beating back the deluge with whaps like a brave metronome.

Had I lost her? Which way had she gone?

I braked hard, cut the wheel, managed to complete a turn without sideswiping a huge, dripping oak

I sat hunched over the wheel, trying to find the truck

through all the chaos. Unreasonable fear tightened the muscles of my arms and shoulders—hell, every muscle of my body—as I fought against the imaginings of how my parents had died under these same insane conditions.

Then I caught a glimpse of what had to be the truck's lights probing erratically through the downpour and woods ahead. She too must have gotten lost. Seconds later, the truck itself came sliding, yawing a little from its speed as if in slow motion, high beams slicing wedges out of the wet night. Brake lights flashed. Headlamps arched among the overgrowth.

She tried to do two things at once—steer the truck in another direction and fire the big revolver back at me. Lightning struck a nearby tree like an atomic bomb.

Our vehicles skidded together and I felt myself flung free from the Kaiser as it spun off road. I landed with a whomp on the side of a hill that was already soaked from the rainfall. I slid farther down and through the wetness, skidding on my side. Easing to a stop, I immediately tried to clamber back up, but the soaked soil gave way. I slipped on ooze and sank deeper into a massive flow of mud.

The rain had shifted the contours of the earth beneath my knees and hands. The mud built up around me, carrying me farther down the hill, as I heard a deep, rumbling explosion and saw a hot, yellow fireball billow up from the other side of the raised highway. The ground shook like a wet dog and more mud rolled down the ridge at me in waves, covering my arms, legs and chest. In another minute, I'd be buried in the oncoming mudslide.

I yelled for help, knowing the rattle of the rain on the trees would drown me out. The lightning flashed again, this time with a tint of red and the thunder that gave a long scream.

The mud cascaded to my face, ice cold. I wriggled violently within its clammy hold, called out again at the top of my lungs, and sank farther in the quicksand. Muck in my eyes. A blur of red. A deep breath and I went under to meet the worms.

CHAPTER 25

Beep-beep.

A sputnik flew through the night sky high above my head.

I tried to remember the last time I'd been in so much pain and couldn't come up with anything older than a few days ago. It struck me that I was becoming addicted to pain, or Darvon, or both. I vowed to switch to straight aspirin, if I had any future. Then I drifted back to where the pain couldn't find me.

Beep-beep.

Patrolman Williams wobbled like bad reception on a cheap Japanese TV and finally came into focus. He raised my soiled sports coat and Hawaiian shirt—one in each hand. "Surf's up, dude."

It took me a second to realize he was not part of a dream and the beeping was one of those hospital monitors attached to several leads on my chest and the side of my neck.

I forced my throat to crack, "Water," and he stuck a paper straw between my lips. I raised my head, gulped in a mouthful of cool salvation, coughed, and rested back into a damp pillow.

Beep-beep.

"Welcome back," Williams said. "Didn't anyone ever tell you can't hang ten on a mudslide?"

This guy was trying to be funnier than me. I couldn't let that happen. "Cowa-bonga."

He grinned. "Yeah, you're going to be all right." He checked his watch. "I got a couple of seconds. Want to tell me your side of what happened?"

"You go first."

To express his intelligence, he cleared his throat. "Well, we found the remains of an exploded vehicle down the gully where you almost took a dirt nap."

I grunted to show that I was intelligent, too.

He flipped a page on his clipboard. All cops had clipboards. They issued them with badges and guns at the training schools. "In any event, the driver is dead and scattered all over the hillside. We think it's a woman."

"Juliette DeLibre. Actress. Real last name is Fayard."

"Might be able to confirm that once we get a print

off a half of hand we found stuck up a tree limb."

My vital-signs monitor kept right on beeping. I shifted my weight and found that it was possible to sit up without anything falling off. "Can you kill that beeping noise?"

He shook his head. "Want me to shoot it?" He was obviously enjoying my misery. "There was another body—male this time, up at that ranch house. Two .44 slugs in it. Probably a match for the gun found in the truck wreckage." He snapped the clip on his board for emphasis. "The LAPD called us up there to investigate. That you're doing?"

I nodded and eased a leg over the side of the bed, still staying in one piece. It felt pretty good, considering. I decided to try for a complete, long sentence. "She was planning to ram the gates at Edwards Air Force Base and drive the truck full of explosives into a tank of poison gas that's supposed to be there."

Beep-beep.

"Yeah, sure," he said, taking it all in.

I added emphasis by saying, "Let me call the head of security at the base. He needs to know about this."

Williams scratched behind his ear with the non-business end of his ballpoint pen and then pointed to a phone sitting on a table beside my bed.

I got my other leg over and sat there trying to remember the number of Scott's office. A nurse came in and told me I should lie back down. I brushed her off and dialed, getting someone on the base who could connect me with the head of security.

While I waited, Williams asked the nurse, "Can we get some coffee in here? And maybe some breakfast? He's doing quite well."

She went "humph" and left, as Colonel Scott came on the line. I filled him in on what had happened and Williams listened to my end of the conversation, making notes along the way.

When I'd finished, I tried standing and felt pretty good about it, considering. I had a few new aches, but everything seemed to be in working condition.

Colonel Scott had asked a few quick questions during my dissertation and then stayed quiet at the end of the line for a long time. It felt like a freeze frame moment in a silent movie, except for the beeping.

"Are you recording this?" he finally asked.

I sighed, reached down, and yanked the power cord from the socket. "No, it's just some hospital equipment. I've shut it off."

"You say there's a patrolman there with you. Let me talk to him."

I took a few trial steps in my bare feet and handed the phone to Williams. It was a rerun of the scene I'd had at Parker Center. The law officer listened, his jaw gradually tightening. While I unstuck the wires from my body, he rubbed the back of his neck, glaring at me so hard that I expected smoke to come out of his ears. A blind man could tell he was angry. I concentrated on doing something really tough—switching from the hospital gown to my limp, yet colorful vacation ensemble. I guessed that someone had a tried to launder it during the night, for which I was appreciative to no end. My shoes were still somewhat of a mess, but the next time I checked into a hospital, I hoped it would be a place as swell as Palmdale General.

The nurse came back with a tray of coffee and heavenly-smelling scrambled eggs.

Somehow, in the middle of his phone conversation, the patrolman's expression softened, and I think he started seeing me in a new light. Finally, he nodded and handed me back the receiver, gesturing for a signature on some yellow paperwork. "Don't let me catch you back here in my jurisdiction, Mr. Wade. Three strikes and you're out." He gave me a one-finger salute and left the room.

I ignored him, wolfed down the breakfast, and put the phone back to my ear to listen to Scott tell me I'd been remanded into his custody under my own recognizance and that I needed to report to him on base within twenty-four hours.

"Will do, sir," I said. "And thanks for the cover with the local cops."

"Your problems are federal now," he said and hung up before I could say, "So are yours."

Through the curtained window, I could see the blue

morning sky. At least one bad storm had passed from my life and I was still able to appreciate the sunshine. Joyful participation? Maybe, except in the last week I'd been shot at, beaten up, played and betrayed, nearly exploded, hung, and drowned—in mud, yet. My clothes, car, and bank account were just about ruined, and on top of everything else Suzi had been shot rescuing me. I wasn't a total failure, but I was the next worst thing to it.

What I'd wanted all along was to solve this murder like a real investigator and prove my worth to Mr. P, Lex, Walt, and practically everyone else I'd ever known, including Stan Wade. But way too much had happened and I still couldn't make sense of it all.

A cloud passed over the sun and the room darkened to match my mood. I sighed. *At least this time, I'm not going to think about ending it all.* Instead, I'd start right away looking for a new line of work. Something I'd be good at. Something like…like finding my car.

ೞೞ

The doctors didn't like my being up and around. We argued as we walked the halls, checking to see if we were healthy and sane. After a few tests and further conversation, I arranged for them to mail a bill to my office, saying that I had to leave for a "governmental meeting of international importance." They were still disgruntled, but seemed impressed enough to release me.

During our blabbing, I learned from them that Suzi was still there at the Palmdale facility, recovering. That little fact changed my immediate plans.

The California HP had hauled my car to the hospital lot, so I went and found my empty gun jammed under the passenger seat where it had fallen during the collision.

I tossed it into the Kaiser's trunk and found something I needed wedged between the spare tire and my Dodger ball cap. I dusted it off and carried it back to Suzi.

I found her up and dressed, when I rapped knuckles on the open door of her room and came in to greet her. I almost gave her a hug and stopped when she pulled back.

The bullet had nicked her right lung, but she was healing quickly. Still, she looked like Christmas morning to me, her shining silver hair combed back, her blue eyes alight. "Standy." She smiled. "You look worse than I feel."

"I feel worse than I look," I said. "And I think we have a solid lead on Johnny's killers. I can fill you in on the details when you're feeling better."

"I already know," she said. "The police told me that they found his body at the bottom of some place west of here, called Bouquet Reservoir. They sent a team of divers down and found other bodies too and the remains of wrecked cars. George's task force at the LAPD is going to go after Reliance Management now for its connections to racketeering."

"That's—that's great news. Finally, someone's making some progress."

"I can fill *you* in on the details when *you're* feeling better." She snickered. "How's your air force case progressing?"

I looked down at my shoes, which were still a mess. "It's stalled out, temporarily," I said. "I had a good lead, but—it didn't work out."

Suzi could always read me like the *Sunday Times*. "Was she pretty?"

I got out the crumpled photostat of Juliette from my wallet and handed it to her. "As it turned out, this woman and her brother were Soviet agents."

"Were?"

"They're both gone now."

"Do I detect that you and she…"

I let it hang there.

She studied the picture and looked up. "She's an actress, right?"

"Uh, yeah. Right."

"I think she came to Reliance once with a guy who looks a little like you, except for his mustache. She was very pretty. You cared for her, didn't you? I can tell from the way you're acting."

I was uncomfortable with her comments and tried to hide the truth. "Offhand, I'd say she dated a lot of guys—for various reasons."

"Oh, Standy—"

I rushed to discuss something, anything, else and handed her the thing I'd taken from the trunk of my car. "Here," I said. "This is something I've been meaning to give you for a long time." She accepted the copy of "Red Wind" that I'd appropriated from Captain Taffe's bedroom. So sue me. "The stories are a little old, but they're still good. Something to read while you're recovering."

She turned the book over and fanned the pages.

I continued to rush ahead, feeling like something wasn't clear. "Do you remember when we were kids at the ranch and I sprained my ankle? You asked me the other day what made me want to—"

I watched as she moved the book so it was behind her back. "Yes, I remember. But right now I have something important to share with you."

I swallowed. "Go on."

"George has proposed marriage."

I kept my face very still. "Well—swell. That's swell."

"He's been very sweet. Coming here each day to see that I'm getting the best treatment."

For the first time, I noticed the flowers in her room that I had not sent. My head started feeling numb.

"I know that it's sudden and all, Standy, but—" she quickly added.

I think I smiled. "Ah—look, Suzi. My allergies are kicking in. You wouldn't mind if I went away and came back later, would you?"

"No. No, not at all." She played along. "Now that you mention it, your eyes *do* look like they're going to water. You should see a doctor about that."

"Good idea," I said, backing toward the door. "I hear they have a few lying around this place. I'll give you a call in a couple days, Suzi. Promise." I could feel my heart in my chest. "You know how to reach me—if you need to."

She nodded pertly with smiling eyes, as I turned away, gulping air like a decked mackerel.

CHAPTER 26

I went back and sat in the car again. It wasn't the best thing to do, but it was the next natural place to go, miserable or not. At least, my gun was empty. I felt pretty much the same way. And tired and stiff and sore—in five different places.

A wave of nausea rolled over me as sat there staring at the long horizon, thinking that I could almost see the curvature of the Earth. My tongue thickened and I swallowed warm saliva as the wave rolled away without taking me with it.

The phone under the dashboard caught my eye and, God help me, I decided to try and call Norman. I needed someone to talk to and he was always a dependable distraction. Maybe it would knock the gloom out of me.

At times, Norman was as goofy as any B-western sidekick. Unlike Andy Devine, or Gabby Hayes, he was a real person, however, and he always gave me a different point of view. I realized that I liked the guy, because he never seemed to stop trying.

I'd never confessed any troubles to him before, but now the time seemed right. He surprised me by answering on the second ring and I started the conversion by telling him I intended to drop the case and maybe the whole profession. He surprised me again by not interrupting while I ranted on.

"Look, Mr. Wade," he finally said. "You know I read a lot of science fiction, right? But the case you're on, that's science fact. It's the future. *Our* future, and you need to make it come out right. It's important to a lot of people."

"Not to me, Norman. And not to anyone I know."

"Don't say that," he shot back under a wave of static from the tenuous phone connection. "I know I'm sometimes paranoid. I know they call me Weirdo Weirick behind my back, but I'm certain about this. There's a lot of phony stuff here in Hollywood, but this is real. This is the right stuff."

"Listen. You don't get it. I just don't care anymore."

"About what?"

"About dead test pilots. About solving mysteries. About just about everything."

He took a thoughtful bite out of that information.

"Those test pilots you're working with will be the next generation's heroes. Don't you know that, as mankind reaches for the stars, those guys will extend the American dream? From now on, kids everywhere won't want to be cowboys or firemen anymore. They'll look up at the stars and want to be astronauts. You understand?"

I was astounded to find myself nodding in agreement and astonished to find that this insight was coming from, of all people, Norman. "Okay. Yes. I guess."

"You can solve this, Mr. Wade. I know you can. You're a terrific detective, like Stu Bailey, Richard Diamond, or that Mike Shayne guy."

"Oh, God. Not him."

"Go over your notes. Review the clues, like you always do."

I had forgotten about what I'd written down in my notebook. I patted my jacket pocket and found that the hospital had put everything back after attending to my dirty clothes. "You know, Norm. Maybe, you're on to something." The book was hard to flip through and a few pages were stuck together, but some of my jottings were still legible. "Thanks, buddy, for the advice and the talk. You're a pretty good detective, yourself."

More crackling bit my eardrum. I thought he said, "Or author."

"That, too." Scanning the notes, I began to re-imagine the case with fresh eyes, as if I were reading a mystery novel. "Thanks again."

"You're welcome, of course." Then he stunned me again. "When life hands you a lemon, make a martini."

"You've got a deal," I said with admiration.

"So you'll read my new chapters, when you get back?"

I fired up the car's engine and told my faithful side-kick—scratch that—friend, "Bring 'em on."

☙☙☙

The bone-dry heat of the desert made the air jittery and the sky crystalline blue. The intense solar glare as I approached Edwards made me squint, wishing for a pair of those aviator sunglasses.

Once on base, the first person I saw was Major Kirkman, who was overseeing the construction of an out-door raised platform with decorative bunting and sound system.

The X-15 was parked behind the stage, its black fuselage and short wings shining in the rays of the sun. He hailed me and I pulled the battered Kaiser over to where he stood in his sweat-stained fatigues.

"Hello, Major." I gestured at the rows of chairs and a tent that was being erected next to the stage. "What's all this?"

"Just a little on-base ceremony for the final selection of the Mercury Seven astronauts," he said, wiping perspiration from his eyebrows. "Many of the candidates will be here later today to see if they've been selected."

"Lucky Seven, eh? You guys don't miss a beat for showmanship."

He grinned and looked to the southwest. The more I saw of the major, the more he reminded me of that guy on *Whirlybirds*, Ken Tobey. "Hollywood is just over those mountains," he said. "This is the real world here."

"So I understand. Sort of the real stuff, eh?"

"Something like that." He shrugged. "Have you come with proof of Taffe's suicide?"

Now that I was sitting here in the sun, I started sweating, too. "I'm still not convinced that it was suicide. The security on this base stinks. A lot of people could have been involved."

"Colonel Scott's not going to like hearing that. He's already pissed at you for something."

Another sonic boom pounded around us, but I'd grown used to them. "I'm headed there now."

He raised his chin. "Mind if I come along? I need to know if this is settled before the start of the ceremony."

"Hop in."

We drove to Building E and I endured another quick security check, while Kirkman confirmed that the security officer was in and would see us.

"You're in a world of shit, mister," Colonel Fielding Scott barked at me after we'd entered the office and closed the door. The blocky, blond man reached down and came up with his pipe pointed at me like it was a loaded automatic. It was a good show that probably always worked to make the other guy uncomfortable, but I wasn't buying intimidation today.

I plunked down in one of his interview chairs to show him I didn't care. Kirkman looked on.

"You've put this program in jeopardy by not finding conclusive proof of Taffe's suicide." A razor burn on his chin started to glow red. "Plus, you've had me interrupt security operations to run cover for you with the local constabulary."

"The security on this base is a bad joke," I told him. "The guards at the gate don't double check or even record license plate numbers. Hell, their guns aren't even loaded." The pipe in his hand lowered a bit, so I went on. "The communists know all about your stockpile of poison gas and are bold enough to think they could plow right through the gates and blow things up."

"We're constantly improving our base security. We execute a twelve-point program daily to—"

"And you let key personnel, including Taffe who was unmarried, go and live off base, where they can be accessed by undercover agents of the USSR. Colonel Scott, you sir, in my opinion, should be shot." I heard Kirkman behind me stifling a response.

Scott, in front of me, glared little daggers like in a Tex Avery cartoon, but put down his killer cherry-wood.

"Look," I said, "it's been a hell of a week. Maybe I went too far with that last remark."

Scott glanced over at the photo of his wife and daughter.

Kirkman came around to my right side. "Can you tell us what you've found out about Taffe's death? We need to know before we make—" He gestured at a scale model of the black X-15 in a support base on Scott's desk. The superjet appeared to be blasting off from between an intercom box and a wire "out" basket. More publicity. More showmanship.

"Have a seat, Roger," Scott said. "Let's get this cleared up."

"Okay," I said. "Let's." The two officers sat and I rolled out what I thought I knew. "As much as it rains on your parade, gentlemen, I say that Taffe was murdered." Kirkman screwed up his mustache and opened his mouth, but I stopped him by raising my voice. "There's no proof that he wasn't. And, furthermore, it wasn't the protestors or the commies and probably not anyone at Reliance Management or the Mob. He could only have been killed by someone here on the base."

Scott looked nervous. "Assuming that's the case, why was he killed?"

That question, I figured I knew the answer to. "Not because of the Mercury Project," I assured them. "Not because of the space race, the Russians, or organized crime."

"Then…" Kirkman said.

"Taffe had been compromised by a Hollywood actress who was actually a Soviet spy. He had fallen in love with her and was preparing to propose marriage. But she had no motive to kill him, because his death would have cut off her source of classified information about your operations here."

Scott glanced at Kirkman and then back at me. "And you know this how?"

"I know it from you two," I said, thinking that this would be an excellent moment to light up a Lucky Strike, dammit. "When you sent me off to find incriminating evidence at Taffe's apartment, I discovered a listening device in the cabinet under his kitchen sink. But it would never have worked properly there in that enclosed location, so I began to suspect it was planted as a false lead to make Taffe seem guilty and perhaps eventually suicidal." It seemed to me that Scott's eyes narrowed a fraction, but I couldn't be sure, so I went on. "The soviets wouldn't have been so dumb as to plant a bug that wouldn't work, so I wondered who knew I'd go there and would probably find it."

Out beyond the office windows, a jet engine roared. Behind me, I could hear the clacking of typewriters through the closed door. The air conditioner began to hum and I wondered how Scott got any work done with all this noise.

He started fiddling again with his pipe, a touch of hardness around his mouth. "I don't understand. This is nothing but conjecture."

"At that point, I couldn't figure it out either," I said, "but then someone sent me a message by telephone at my office. It was essentially a warning to 'butt out.' Only a few people connected with the case knew my current address and could have called there to leave such a message." I turned to Kirkman. "The business card I gave you here in this office had my old address, so I discounted both of you, but later I found out from my client that you'd both spoken with him and thus had an opportunity to ask about my current contact information."

Kirkman made a show of looking at his watch. "Can we get to the point, please?"

I adjusted my weight in the chair and studied his face. "The point is, Taffe was killed because of a common motive that I encounter all the time: jealousy. One of you two were also Juliette's lover. The one who has no photos in his office of a spouse or a wedding ring on his finger. The one who was seen at Reliance headquarters with Juliette by a trustworthy witness. The one who looked a lot like me, except he has a mustache."

Kirkman stood suddenly and I matched his move. "So you think I killed Taffe? That's ridiculous."

"Is it?" Scott said around the pipe in his teeth.

"Come on, Fielding, you know me better. I was your wingman when we flew F-86s in Korea."

Scott put down his pipe. "We found the original security film that you hid in the media room. You should have destroyed it, Roger."

"But I did," Kirkman said.

I was impressed with Colonel Scott's bluff and started moving in on his PR man.

Kirkman realized what he'd said and stepped back.

"You didn't just want him dead," I said, "you wanted him disgraced—in her eyes."

He pulled a two-shot Derringer from his pants pocket and fired at me. Firing any kind of gun while pulling it from your pants is a tricky, untrained move. I went down to the floor the second I saw it come out and he fired high, about where my head should have been.

I almost grabbed for the X-15 model to throw at him like a fat dart, but I knew I couldn't reach it in time to keep him from firing at me again.

"Halt!" Scott called from behind his desk where he fired a .45 Colt and put an end to the action. Kirkman slammed back against the office door from the bullet's impact to his arm and shivered, dropping to the floor.

I kicked the gun from his open palm and turned to Scott. "Much obliged, Colonel. I can't believe you just shot Smilin' Jack."

He lowered his smoking sidearm. "I can't believe he was carrying a 'pepper-box' in his pants."

We grinned at each other to relieve the tension as office workers and MPs rushed in.

CHAPTER 27

Where did he think he was going?" Walt said. "I don't know. It's an enclosed military base. Hundreds of physically fit air force men would have been all over him in minutes."

"Maybe he has a death wish."

Phone static bit my ear as I drove under high-tension wires. "Maybe. But when I finally worked it all out and pegged him for the killer, there was no way I was going to let him get away."

"I've read your report. You did the absolute right thing, Stan."

"Then answer me one question, Walt. You're a businessman in the entertainment industry. Why are *you* involved in all of this?"

"A contract is a contract."

"What's that supposed to mean?"

"Did you ever do anything that you couldn't talk about?" he asked.

"All the time."

"Then just settle for this—the good work you accomplish for me undercover is important and I can't get it done any better way. You do things and go places that I can't and I appreciate you for it. Like I told you before, the work is absolutely vital and I absolutely cannot discuss it over the phone."

"Okay. I'm absolutely glad you like my work, Walt. But it wasn't just me. I had plenty of help from a number of close associates and I can't put them at risk."

"Then you can imagine *my* position. This work is not easy, but it's essential. From now on, if you like, you can consider yourself on permanent retainer, but mum's the word with your associates."

I don't think he got my point, but I didn't press it. Instead, before hanging up, I used the non-committal line Cindy had given me a week or so ago: "Sounds charming. I'll get back to you."

It was Thursday, April ninth as I steered the Kaiser off the San Diego freeway and caught Route 94 West near Balboa Park. It had rained April showers earlier that morning across southern California and, now, a cool breeze blow through the car's open windows.

At 11 a.m. pacific time, I caught the nationwide radio broadcast of a press conference in Washington DC. The ceremony was hosted by NASA to introduce the country to the new Mercury Seven astronauts. One of the reporters there asked if the seven men were ready to ride rockets into the unknown. All seven eagerly answered, "Yes."

The Mercury Seven had been selected back on April first, but not officially notified until the next day, so it wouldn't seem to them like a cruel joke.

I had wrapped up the case that same day and gotten back to the boat for a welcome rest. Throughout the following week, I'd taken time to heal my battered body and cleaned up my battered car. I'd relaxed and fished a little off the stern of the cruiser. I'd written and delivered a full report to Walt in order to get paid for all the hell he'd put me through.

I'd checked in at my office in the Derby and visited with Cindy, learning that Jimmy had been expressing an interest in becoming a private eye when he grew up. She put an immediate stop to that idea, urging him back to something safer and saner. So, now he wanted to be a spaceman.

I had made a point to treat Norman to lunch, thanking him again for his help and encouragement when I had needed it. As requested, I dutifully read through the new chapters of his science fiction novel, understanding little of it, and selfishly hoped he wouldn't give up his day job.

This morning, during the long drive south from LA,

I'd conferred with Walt on the car phone and then let my mind continue to unwind.

The traffic cruising along the San Diego freeway didn't seem to bother me like it did back home. I allowed myself to ponder the fact that there were more cars in Los Angles than there were stars in Hollywood. Stars whose careers flared brightly as they rose in the public's consciousness before falling and fading away. But Taffe was a real star who never got a chance to rise, never got a chance to be recognized or appreciated. Soon, the real stars of the space program would outshine the celluloid ones of tinsel town. Albert Taffe would not be among them. Rather, he would rest in an unnoticed grave somewhere in Iowa—a fallen star in the heart of the American heartland.

I took the Market Street exit off 94 West and drove through a quiet San Diego bedroom community. In the 3000 block on the south side of the street, I found the entrance to the Mount Hope Cemetery where another star had fallen to earth. When I pulled into the gravel parking lot, I caught sight of a blonde woman getting out of a taxi. She wore a plum-colored pillbox hat with a black veil pinned up on top, and a purple sundress printed with green and red flowers.

She stepped into the cool air after the morning rain, and waved at me. I realized that I'd always been fascinated by that slightly pug nose over her straight, white teeth. I got out of the Kaiser and walked to meet her.

"How did you know I'd be here, or even in San Die-go, for that matter?"

"I'm a detective," Suzi said. "You big dope."

I shook my head in mock protest. "I am not. I'm the large economy size."

She looked up, appealing to heaven. "I called your office and Cindy told me you were headed down here. I caught a morning flight and then a cab to this address."

I glanced behind me to make sure we weren't on *Candid Camera.*

The breeze fluttered her bangs. "You know, Standy, I think that girl has a minor crush on you. You should consider asking her out."

I still felt a little dizzy from finding her here. "Oh, you think I should, huh? Well, maybe I'm playing hard to get."

She smiled and stood nearer. Chanel No. 5 again. "More like, hard to take."

We paid off the cabby and took our time walking into the memorial park, past the final resting places. The sun warmed us from the cool wind. The grass was newly clipped and brilliant green. In the distance, at least one bird, maybe two, sang happily.

Suzi spoke in a quiet voice. "I read the book you gave me. Do you know where his grave is?"

"I think I can find it."

We walked together until we reached a spot where the ground had been recently turned. The small bouquet placed next to the simple plaque in the earth had already withered. I raised my eyes and scanned the nearby horizon to the fenced enclosure. No mausoleums, no headstones or no crosses. Just a few skinny trees, the gravel walkways, and mowed grass. Again, I had forgotten to bring flowers.

Suzi quoted Chandler in a hushed voice. "What did it matter where you lay once you were dead?"

"Geez, I was going to say that. Is there nothing you don't know?"

"He was only a writer, huh?"

I looked down at the dirt. "He was too good to be only a writer."

She sniffed and hung on my elbow. "When you sprained your ankle back at the dude ranch in '46, you read his story "Red Wind" in an old *Dime Detective* pulp." I nodded, marveling silently at how much she knew about me. She sighed. "When you gave me the book the other day at the hospital, I remembered seeing you with that old magazine back then."

I felt the urge to tell her everything. "That story made me think for the first time that I might like to become a detective. Later in September, I saw Bogart in *The Big Sleep* and was completely taken away by the idea."

"I know." She shrugged. "And I guess I sort of followed your lead."

There was so much blue in the sky and her eyes that

I almost tipped over. "Well, here's something you don't know. The 'D' that you keep adding to the end of my name—it's my middle initial. And long before Chandler wrote novels about Philip Marlowe, he first wrote short stories about a PI—"

"Named John Dalmas, I know. You're such a sentimental little boy, Standy."

I just stood there.

"Come on." She tugged at my sleeve. "I'm hungry."

As we walked back to my car, I asked, "What happened to George and his proposal?"

She looked straight ahead. "You probably don't realize it, but I've always felt that you live a life that is methodical and plodding, but unrelenting."

"Me?"

"That's why I eventually came to you for help finding out what happened to Johnny. I realize now that part of the reason he died was because he was over-confident, impulsive, and slightly dangerous. George is the same way. He's sweet, but—"

"Be still my foolish heart."

She gave that a light giggle. "And, you're funny, too. I think I can live with that."

I stopped our stroll and took her in my arms. We came together, kissing warmly, and then made a mess of it by laughing in the graveyard.

⌘

On the road back to LA, the phone buzzed. I wasn't certain that the damn thing could receive in-coming calls.

Cindy's voice played in my ear. "Norman mixed or patched me through to you, Stan. Is 'mixed' the right word? You need to get back here right away."

"Yeah, that Norman. He makes a mean martini." I hoped he heard that. "What's so urgent?"

Suzi stuck her tongue out at me and started fiddling with the dial of the AM radio.

Cindy's voice started breaking up from interference. "George Reeves wants to hire you. You know— Superman?" Static buzzed and the line went dead.

Suzi found a local station playing pop tunes.

I pushed down on the gas and headed home while the Chordettes joyfully sang, "Lollipop, lollipop, oh lolly, lolly, lolly…"

I loved my job.

The Facts Behind the Fiction

The expansion of Disneyland, including the Submarine Voyage and Monorail, opened to the public on June 14, 1959.

Hawaii became our fiftieth state on August 21, 1959 and Warner Brothers premiered its TV detective series *Hawaiian Eye* six weeks later.

The Dodgers won the pennant and the World Series in 1959.

Gregory Peck starred in *On the Beach* late in 1959, an anti-war, post-nuclear holocaust film.

Gordon "Gordo" Copper went into space in 1963 and had the dubious honor of being the first American to sleep there.

The Lagoon del Rey was dredged a year later and is now the site of the world-famous Marina del Rey.

Mickey Cohen was charged, tried, and sent to Alcatraz for tax evasion in 1961. He died in his sleep of supposed stomach cancer complications in 1976.

PKD (Philip K. Dick) went on to write several influential SF novels, including *The Man in the High Castle* and *Do Androids Dream of Electric Sheep*. He passed away in 1982, firmly believing that the government had been spying on him.

Tony Perkins made sixty-six films, including three follow-ups to Hitchcock's *Psycho*, finally joining his mother and others in the great beyond in 1992.

Ed "Kookie" Byrnes recorded a hit record about his famous comb later in 1959. He eventually returned to Warner Brothers and *77 Sunset Strip*, but never made it big in films or other TV programs.

Jack Benny is still with us in DVD, VHS, and OTR. He is currently 39.

In an attempt to minimize the potential for spy-talk in the bedroom, the Mercury Project instituted a regulation that all astronauts be married men. It didn't work.

Thus far, all attempts to put a time machine in a car have failed.

Months after the events described here, on September nineteenth, Nikita Khrushchev visited the Twentieth Century Fox Studios, where *Can-Can* was being filmed. There, he wanted to know why he had not been allowed to go to Disneyland. Nobody would give him a straight answer, but the reason was that someone in Nikita's party planned to use the opportunity to kill Walt. I was on the Fox lot that day and so was Walt in disguise wearing an eye patch—but that's another story.

If you enjoyed

STARFALL

Turn the page for a preview of

SUPERFALL

the next book in the Stan Wade Series

Coming from John Hegenberger and
Black Opal Books in Late Summer 2016

PROLOGUE

One day...June 18, 1959:

Look, I'm dead already," George Reeves whispered. "Can't we leave it at that?"

I hated my work. Well, not all the time. Just when I got a headache from dealing with bullheaded movie and TV stars.

Reeves sat in the booth in the Brown Derby restaurant on Wilshire, hidden under a heavy beard, dark glasses, and a darker wig that made him look like a dark Harpo Marx. A sketch of the real Harpo hung on the wall behind him among the rows of Hollywood caricatures.

The blonde seated next to him patted his hand gently. "You don't have to whisper, baby."

Her name, I'd been told, was Naomi Lugosi, but I figured that, like so many things in the Hollywood of the '50s, it was staged. Her hair was blonde, long, and flowing, making her appear like Veronica Lake, except I could see both of her dark tarnished eyes.

My hair, on the other hand, needed a trim and had a white streak that ran from my forehead to my crown. I was a bit too thin to be considered ruggedly handsome, with brown eyes, five foot eleven, a habit of interrupting, and a persistent sinus condition from our wonderful LA air.

"I'm just tired of people mourning over me," George said, "like I was a god…or something."

Seated across from him and girl, I shrugged and commented, "You *were* sort of a god to millions of kids, you know."

Reeves, of course, had been famous for his portrayal of the Man of Steel on the *Adventures of Superman* TV program.

"But I was a joke to adults. No one over the age of eleven took me seriously. Typecast into kiddieland. Do you know what Disney did to my role in that wagon train movie? He cut me down to a walk on." George scratched under his wig and above his left ear. "I think this rug is giving me head lice."

I knew full well what had happened to Reeves's part in Walt's *Westward Ho, the Wagons*. During the preview screenings, you could actually hear the audience gasp when George came on screen, and the hushed word, "Superman," rolled around the audience like muted thunder.

"Not to mention what happened in *From Here to Eternity*," the big actor in the trench coat complained while he fiddled irritably with the salt shaker in our booth.

The same unwanted recognition had occurred at the pre-screening of the Columbia Studios' Burt Lancaster feature. George's meaty part was cut down to nothing, because audiences recognized him the second he appeared and the director knew that it broke the film's narrative flow.

It was all too much for Reeves. He became totally fed up with acting and, in the end, took the easy way out when the circumstances presented themselves. He had come to me weeks earlier, looking to hire me to help with some of those same circumstances. On top of everything else, George had gambling issues and local mobsters, like LA's finest hood, Mickey Cohen, and his known associates were starting to send not-so veiled threats about paying up.

The blonde Lugosi lit a Camel with tiny, butane lighter. I didn't know much about the lady, but George vouched for her when we'd set up our meeting today, here at the hat-shaped restaurant. The plan was to see if he and I could identify a small-time hood who had been muscling Bob Cobb, the restaurant's owner, into offering patrons off-track betting 'under the tables' at the Brown

Derby. Horseracing. Derby. Get it? In the city of angles, everybody has one.

George looked at Naomi, his face a scowl. "This was not part of our original deal, you know. I'm supposed to be on a train east to Pittsburgh."

The longhaired blonde patted his hand again. "The Bureau has it covered, baby. We spot this creep and we'll have the connection we need. Then, you can go on to your new life."

There was a firm assured tone in her voice that made me understand that the Lady Lugosi wasn't just any dumb blonde. I studied her for a moment. "I get it now. You're his handler. You've got his back covered."

She smiled broadly at me. "Baby, I've got his whole body."

George grinned and pulled down his shades, winking at me the way he used to at the end of a TV episode.

"Bullshit." I laughed, sitting back in the padded booth. To our right, another TV actor named Something Coburn was enjoying lunch with director Bud Boetticher.

The undercover girl with the phony name cooed, "Georgie, or should I call him Ralph now, is faster than a speeding bullet. And I'm no Lois Lane."

She was no Gracie Allen, either, as they sat there looking deeply into each other's eyes and ignoring me.

I was here this bright summer's day to perform one act that would help two clients: George and Mr. Cobb. George had asked me to help once again with his mob and gambling problems—problems so severe that they caused him to go into an FBI program that promised to protect him with a new identity, if he'd bear witness against local racketeers.

Mr. Cobb needed, and expected, my help, because lately I'd been working out of a temporary office in the crowded, noisy rear of his restaurant. Cobb kept me on retainer to "police" the premises in general and lean specifically on any freeloading Hollywood talent who wouldn't pay their bar bills. We'd had this arrangement for several months now and I'd almost forgotten how much I owed him, until he told me about the racing tout.

The Derby was a classy place to meet clients and prospects and I got plenty of eats while running my Professional Investigation business out of a cubbyhole office back where all the other employees clocked in and washed their hands. It wasn't what I'd imagined when I'd started out as a PI years ago, but like George, I'd taken the easy way out when circumstance presented themselves. Also my old office in the Farraday building had been torched.

As it turned out, the same race tout whom Mr. Cobb had wanted muscled off the premises was also the "creep" that the blonde FBI agent had wanted identified for Mob connections. When the creepy tout entered the front door of the restaurant, I noticed right away the small, quick movements and the thin face and pointed nose. He made a show of scanning the tables and booths from the front of the room and then strolled over to speak with Tennessee Ernie Ford who was dining with, as it happened, Dinah Shore.

The BD was known for the celebs who graced its tables and the framed sketches of same that adorned its walls. I didn't think Ford or Shore were the gambling type, and it appeared that I was right, because the little man soon shoved off with a wave and headed for the sandwich shop that adjoined the restaurant proper. Something in the gesture seemed familiar. I'd seen it before, recently.

"That him?" asked the Bela babe.

George and I spoke in unintended unison, "Yep." Then he went on, "They call him Nicky the Nose, because he knows the inside information from the Santa Anita track and how to get a bet down."

I asked, "The nose knows?"

Reeves ignored me. "He has a direct line into Cohen's gambling organization. I think he's related somehow. You track him; you get the Mick."

"Okay," Lady Lugosi said, nudging George and sliding from the booth. "Let's go."

"Wait a minute." I hissed, bringing them to a halt. "Something's wrong here."

George and the woman spoke in unintended unison, "What?"

"You say that guy's with the Mob? I've seen him before and know that he's also a high-level closet commie."

The disguised, dead actor and his blonde handler disappeared before my eyes, and I was sitting across the booth from two concerned and confused individuals, who spoke in unison: "Bullshit!"

I started getting that old headache again.

About the Author

John Hegenberger writes adventure, mystery, science, and horror fiction. Born and raised in the heart of the heartland, Columbus, Ohio, he is the author of *Tripleye* series and the *Stan Wade LA PI* series from Black Opal Books. Father of three, a tennis enthusiast, collector of silent films and OTR, hiker, Francophile, B.A. Comparative Literature, ex-navy, ex-comic book dealer, ex-marketing exec at Exxon, AT&T, and IBM, he has been happily married for over 45 years.

Over the years, he's published two non-fiction books about collecting pop-culture movie memorabilia and comic books and sold half a dozen novels in 2015. Follow his adventures at johnhegenberger.com and have fun.

www.ingramcontent.com/pod-product-compliance
Lightning Source LLC
Chambersburg PA
CBHW060955120726
47910CB00002B/645